SEAL'S ULTIMATE CHALLENGE

ELLE JAMES

TWISTED PAGE INC

SEAL'S ULTIMATE CHALLENGE

TAKE NO PRISONERS BOOK #10

New York Times & *USA Today*
Bestselling Author

ELLE JAMES

EBOOK ISBN: 978-1-62695-159-4

PRINT ISBN: 978-1-62695-160-0

I dedicate this story to the fallen marines and sailor of the senseless slayings at the Tennessee recruiting center. My heart goes out to them and the families they left behind. May they be forever remembered for their selfless dedication to protecting our country.

Elle James

ABOUT THIS BOOK

Injured on a mission gone wrong, Cory "Reaper" Nipton's Navy SEAL career is over. With only one arm, he can't join his fellow teammates, or even his fiancé, the Special Ops helicopter pilot who flew him in and out of harm's way. Relegated to life as a civilian, and angry at his lack of choices, Reaper goes through rehab with a petite, soft-spoken physical therapist with two iron fists. He's forced to face an uncertain future and learn how to live without the use of his right arm.

Ex-cop, Leigha Fields, lost her career due to a gunshot wound that destroyed her knee. Retrained and refitted with different skills, she has reimagined her world, dedicating her life to helping wounded warriors find their way. Until someone from her past seeks revenge. Leigha and Reaper join forces to untangle the mystery and free her from the web of crosshairs aimed squarely at her. In their struggle to find and neutralize the culprit, they realize their own capabilities and how they will fit in their future together.

AUTHOR'S NOTE

SEAL's Ultimate Challenge is from Cory
"Reaper" Nipton's point of view following Book
#1 in the
Take No Prisoners Series
SEAL's Honor (#1)
SEAL'S Desire (#2)
SEAL's Embrace (#3)
SEAL's Obsession (#4)
SEAL's Proposal (#5)
SEAL's Seduction (#6)
SEAL'S Defiance (#7)
SEAL's Deception (#8)
SEAL's Deliverance (#9)
SEAL's Ultimate Challenge (#10)

Visit ellejames.com for more titles and release
dates

For hot cowboys, visit her alter ego Myla Jackson at mylajackson.com

Join Elle James and Myla Jackson's Newsletter at Newsletter

1

Ninety-one, ninety-two, ninety-three. Sweat dripped from every pore of Cory "Reaper" Nipton's body as he did what he could to stay in shape while deployed in Afghanistan and waiting for mission assignment. In his quarters, with his feet hooked beneath the legs of his cot, he counted out six more sit-ups.

The door opened, and Reed Tucker—his teammate, roommate and best friend—stomped inside, scowling.

Reaper completed one more sit-up. One hundred. Pausing in the upright position, he asked, "Have a good run?"

"Hell no," Tuck bit out and pointed to the wadded T-shirt on the floor between the two cots. "Can't you pick up after yourself?"

Reaper crunched a few more sit-ups and stopped. He rose, retrieved the shirt, and stuffed it into his dirty laundry bag hanging from a tent pole.

Tuck was on a tear.

Reaper shrugged and asked, "What bug crawled up your ass?"

"Who said I had a bug up my ass?" Tuck clenched his fists and paced the length of the tent and back, his nostrils flaring, his eyes wild and angry.

The guy looked like he wanted to hit someone. Since Reaper was the closest to him, he backed a step and raised his brows. "Well, if you're not mad about some*thing*, you're mad at some*one*. Let me guess. Is it the commander? Did he ask you to clean the head?"

Tuck snorted and shot a glare at Reaper. "I'm not mad at the commander."

"Then who *are* you mad at? I'm not into twenty questions right now. I have to get to the mess tent before O'Connell." He'd been working on his campaign to win the heart of Captain Delaney O'Connell, the only female helicopter pilot in the 160th Night Stalkers, the bravest, most experienced helicopter unit in the U.S. Army. They had the dangerous task of delivering and recovering Special Operations teams to hostile territory.

Before they'd deployed from Little Creek, Virginia, to Afghanistan, Reaper had asked O'Connell to marry him in a bar, in front of his entire team. She'd put him off, saying she wanted time to think about it. Since then, he'd done everything in his power to sway her thoughts in his direction. "I want to leave a candy bar for the cook to give her as a special treat."

"That's it." Tuck rounded on Reaper, his fists clenched. "That's the reason I'm so jacked up."

Reaper's jaw dropped. "Because of a candy bar? I have another, if you want it."

"No, I don't want your goddamn candy bar. I want you to leave Delaney alone."

Reaper's brows dipped toward the bridge of his nose. "O'Connell? Why? Did the commander find out I was courting her?"

"No. The commander doesn't know anything. But I do, and I want you to stop seeing Delaney."

Reaper had never seen his buddy this wound up before. Especially over a woman.

Ever since BUD/s training, Tuck had been adamant about staying single. A SEAL had no right shackling himself to a woman.

Completely confused by now, Reaper stared at his friend, trying to understand. "Why?"

Tuck shoved a hand through his hair and turned away, mumbling, "Just because I asked you to."

Reaper had a plan. He wanted to be married to O'Connell before he turned thirty. The campaign to win her was in full swing, and he was almost positive he was making headway. He couldn't give up just because Tuck said so. "Sorry, Tuck. That answer isn't good enough."

His friend stood with his back to Reaper. "You're not the right man for her."

Anger flared in his belly, and Reaper clenched his own fists. Now Tuck had pissed him off. "I'm not?" Reaper grabbed Tuck's arm and jerked him around. "Are you saying I'm not good enough? Just because I didn't grow up with a silver spoon in my mouth doesn't make me inferior. I'm a good SEAL, I make a decent living, and I care about her more than I've cared about anyone else in my life."

The muscle in the side of Tuck's jaw ticked. "That's not enough."

"Why?" Reaper crossed his arms and narrowed his gaze. "Give me one good reason why."

"Because..." A red stain rose up Tuck's neck, filling his cheeks. "Just because, damn it! You're not right for her."

"And what made you qualified to be the judge? You've been around her as much as I have. The three of us have been hanging out for the past six months." He jerked a hand toward the door. "I care about her, and I think she cares about me."

Tuck poked a finger into Reaper's chest. "You've never been serious about a woman before."

The poke made the anger flare even hotter inside Reaper.

"You flirt with every female you come in contact with." Tuck went to poke him again

This time, Reaper grabbed his finger. "I'm done with flirting," he said. "O'Connell is the only one for me."

Tuck snatched away his hand from Reaper. "How do you know? Another woman could come along and off you'd go, panting after her. Where would that leave Delaney?"

What kind of question is that? Reaper shook his head. "I'm not going after another woman. I only want O'Connell."

"Damn it, Reaper. What if she doesn't want you?" Tuck stood with his feet planted wide apart, his eyes narrowed, his fists raised and ready.

Tired of the argument and the crazed look in his roommate's eyes, Reaper pulled himself up straight, his chin lifting. "I told you. I'm out to convince her." He poked a finger into his buddy's chest. "Either you're with me, or..." With a shoulder bump, Reaper shoved Tuck. "Stay the fuck out of my way." Moving fast, he left the tent and headed for the mess hall. O'Connell would get her candy bar, and Reaper would be one step closer to sealing the deal with the woman who would be the mother of his children.

"Reaper!" Fish called out from across the dirt road. "Grab Tuck. The Skipper wants us in Ops ASAP."

With a sigh, Reaper turned back to his quarters and stuck his head inside. "Time to rock and roll."

LATER THAT NIGHT, two Black Hawk helicopters flew to their destination. Reaper's only consolation to not having dinner with O'Connell was knowing she was the pilot who would fly them to and from their landing zone outside of the small Afghan village where they'd secure their target and get the hell out.

A hill over from the village, the helicopters hovered above the ground. The SEALs fast-roped to the ground one at a time.

Tuck took point. Reaper had his six, the rest of the team hit the ground and hustled toward the village. This was the same maneuver they'd practiced over and over back in Virginia before being deployed. They could perform this mission with one hand tied behind their backs.

Before they reached the outer walls of the village, gunfire sounded. Tuck and the rest of the team hit the dirt and spent a few tense moments locating the source of the rounds. Reaper glanced through the night vision scope with one eye, the other open to watch for tracer rounds.

A rumbling burst of machine gun fire rippled in the night. After two more tracer rounds, Reaper had his man in his sights and picked him off with a single shot.

Tuck gave a hand signal, and the team was on the move again.

Shouts filled the night air. The people inside the walls were on the alert. Those who were armed would be setting up positions on the rooftops and at the corners of buildings. The SEAL team's job was to neutralize threats and push on to their target. Tuck arrived first, crouched and cupped his hand. Reaper stepped into it and flung himself and his heavy array of weapons to the top of the wall. Lying as flat as he could, he scanned the ground and the rooftops nearest him. So far, the area was clear. He dropped to the ground on the other side and provided cover as, one after the other, his teammates cleared the wall and landed on the ground nearby. The fourth man over stopped at the top, reached back and hauled Tuck up the wall, and they both dropped to the ground on the inside.

Once again, Tuck took point, leading the team through the narrow streets. Reaper hung back, his gaze shooting to the tops of buildings and the rims of the outer walls of mud and stone surrounding the dwellings. The intelligence guys had briefed them on their target, their information gathered from a captured Taliban leader. Tuck would be counting doors to the right location.

At the same time, Team Bravo circled the village to the rear of the building to block anyone attempting to sneak out the back when Team Alpha struck.

A burst of machinegun fire kicked up dust near their feet and halted their progress. Team Alpha pressed their backs to the walls, hugging the shadows, giving the gunner as small a target as possible. The gunfire stopped, and a metal-on-metal clinking sound indicated either the gun had jammed or the shooter was reloading.

Tuck pointed to Reaper then motioned for Big Bird, Fish and Gator to follow. The three men moved past, leaving Reaper to do what he did best.

Inching out into the open, Reaper peered through his night vision goggles and picked up the heat signature of the shooter. He raised his NVGs, leveled his rifle, lined up his target in his scope, and held his breath.

The shooter unjammed his gun and prepared to fire.

Before he could, Reaper caressed his trigger. A single round launched from his rifle, hitting the man between the eyes.

The man expelled air from his lungs in a soft grunt and slumped over his machine gun.

After a deep breath, Reaper hurried to catch up to Tuck and the others.

A couple of yards ahead, Tuck held up a hand. They'd arrived at their target.

The team hunkered low. Reaper took up a position on the corner of a building, scanning the rooftops and the path from which they'd just come. He had the team's six while Tuck got busy with explosives.

Reaper waited, pushing his earlier argument with Tuck out of his mind. No matter how mad he got at Tuck, or Tuck got with him, they would take a bullet for each other. They were part of a team.

A moment later, Tuck ran back to where Reaper was and motioned him to take cover. Tuck checked his watch.

Reaper didn't. His job was to provide cover while Tuck synchronized their efforts with Team Bravo's. They all had to be in their exact places before the party began.

Out of the corner of his eye, Reaper could see

Tuck cover his ears, while he pressed the hand-held detonator.

The explosion shook the ground beneath Reaper's feet. Another blast, a moment later, sounded from the backside of the compound.

Tuck rounded the corner first, Reaper followed. Big Bird and Gator brought up the rear. Ahead, the popping sound of gunfire kicked up dust around their feet and knocked chinks of mud out of the walls. Tuck ducked and rolled into the shadows.

Reaper trained his NVGs at the roof, searching for the sniper.

Tuck, positioned a few feet ahead, had a clearer shot and took him out.

Leaving Fish on the outside of the structure to cover their rear, Tuck, Reaper, Big Bird, and Gator entered through the hole created by the explosives, and spread out.

Team Alpha was to enter through the rear of the structure. Bravo would come through the front door. If they played their cards right, the distraction at the front would allow Team Alpha to secure their target. The trick was to use only enough explosives to penetrate the wall without killing those inside. Intel wanted the man alive for interrogation, which made the SEAL team's job a lot harder.

Tuck affixed C4 to the back wall of the residence, stepped back with the others, and detonated the charge.

With dust still swirling around the hole, Reaper entered first, diving through the crumbled wall. He rolled to a crouch, weapon ready, his finger on the trigger. They'd practiced this maneuver several times stateside at Little Creek, anticipating resistance from within. Most members of the Taliban attended meetings with their leaders, while armed.

In the fog of dust, the first thing that struck Reaper was the room was empty. No guns, no snipers, no Taliban—just rags and empty crates. Had they gotten bad intelligence? Had Tuck counted wrong?

Someone had spray painted lettering on the wall in Pashtu. Reaper didn't have time to stop and translate. He had a job to do. Clear the building, find the Taliban and secure their target. He moved toward the next room. From ahead, he could hear Team Bravo, coming in from the other side.

Behind him, he heard Tuck curse, then yell, "Reaper, don't go—"

Something touched his shin. His mind made the connection and he formed a curse in his mouth, and then the entire room erupted. He was flung through the air. Stunned, his ears ringing, he reached for his weapon, but couldn't find it. Reaper fought to remain conscious. He had to help his team. Someone could have been hurt. From a long way off, he heard the sound of Tuck's voice calling.

"Hey, buddy. Wake up."

Reaper's ears rang with a high-pitched whine, and muffled sounds came to him as if from a thousand miles away. He tried to open his mouth, to reassure Tuck he was all right. No sound came out. Nothing. *I'm here.*

Pressure on his chest and the vast amounts of dust made breathing hard. No matter how much he willed his body to move or his eyes to open, nothing was working. As if his system was jammed and he needed a reboot.

An explosion sounded nearby. *Have to get out.* The mind was willing, but the body wasn't cooperating.

The rumble of voices nearby reassured him.

"Tuck?" A voice called from down a long tunnel. "Tuck?"

Tuck's response came from closer. "I'm here."

"You okay?" the other voice said.

"Yeah." Tuck sounded strained. "But Reaper's down."

Was that why he couldn't move? Reaper tried again to force his mouth and eyes to open.

"Alive?"

By now, Reaper figured the other voice was Big Bird.

"For now," Tuck said.

Just give me a minute. I'll be up and out of this dirt. I just need a minute.

"We're taking rounds and mortars," Big Bird went on. "Team Bravo was hit hard. Two dead, the other three heading back to the LZ."

Dead? Who? Again, Reaper tried to reach for his weapon. *I'll kill the bastards.* No amount of concentration helped. He couldn't wrap his hand around his gun. It probably landed away from him when he'd been thrown.

"Fish and Gator?"

Reaper's concentration faded. He was getting weaker.

"Injured but mobile. Need help getting Reaper out?"

I can stand, Reaper thought. *Just help me to my feet.*

"I'm not sure what injuries he sustained." Tuck paused and then said, "Holy shit. Shine your light over here."

A pale light penetrated Reaper's eyelids. Still, he couldn't open them.

The shuffle of feet sounded close to his head.

Then Big Bird said, "Fuck."

Movement sounded around him. Someone grabbed his right arm and pulled something tight around it. Pain shot through the numbness. Reaper felt himself slipping away.

"We gotta get him out of here," Tuck said, his words terse.

"I know. You go ahead of me." Big Bird's deep voice rumbled through the darkness. "I'm right behind you."

More mortar rounds exploded, shaking the ground beneath them. They had to leave. For the first time since he'd been hit, he realized he might not make it out. Reaper focused, pushing back the inner darkness creeping up on him. When he opened his mouth this time, he was able to push air past his vocal cords. "Tuck." He blinked and opened his eyes. A light shined down in his face, and he squinted against its brightness.

"Yeah, buddy," Tuck said.

"Get out of here," he said, the sound more of a hoarse whisper.

"Not without you."

Reaper sucked in a breath, the effort harder than any training he'd endured in BUD/s. "If I die, take care of Delaney for me, will ya?" He tried to lift his right arm to touch Tuck's arm, but it wasn't working. But his left one did. With his strength fading, he touched Tuck with his left hand. "Promise."

Tuck frowned, a muscle jerking in his jaw.

"Bullshit on all this talk about dying. You're making it out of here alive, so hang on." He bent, grabbed Reaper's left arm, and dragged him over his shoulder in a fireman's carry.

Pain shot through Reaper, and he slipped into that black abyss of unconsciousness.

He faded in and out as his body was jolted and jostled.

Gunfire sounded around him.

"Hang on," Tuck said. "Hang on." The word echoed again and again as he drifted in and out of consciousness.

Through the ringing in his ears, Reaper heard the distant sound of rotor blades beating the air. *Come on, Tuck. Almost there.*

Pain radiated throughout his body, seeming to come from his right arm. He blacked out and woke up, lying on the ground, with something heavy lying over his chest. The sound of gunfire and helicopter rotors filled the air. The pressure on his chest shifted.

Tuck cried out, "No!"

An explosion overhead lit the insides of Reaper's eyelids. He blinked open his eyes to a huge fireball above him, rotor blades breaking away from the fuselage of a helicopter. It fell from the sky, crashing to the ground.

Reaper's last thought before he passed out

was *Delaney*. He woke once more and stared up at the interior of a helicopter.

Fish's face swam before him. Fish was saying something. "He's hanging on…"

The darkness consumed Reaper. He didn't surface again until the familiar thumping sound of rotor blades slowed to a halt.

Hands rolled his body over and back onto a hard board. Pain ripped through him, and he hissed. The next thing he was conscious of was being lifted and carried across the landing pad then settled onto a gurney.

He forced his eyes open and stared up into Delaney's serious face. A huge sense of relief washed over him, pushing the pain to the back of his mind, if only for a moment.

"O'Connell?" He tried to reach out with his right hand, but it wasn't working, so he raised his left hand.

Delaney grasped it. "Yeah, Cory, I'm here."

"You never answered." He coughed, something thick and warm dribbled from the side of his mouth. "You gonna marry…me?" His eyelids were too heavy to keep open. He let them drift closed, and he waited for her response.

"Sure, Cory. I'll marry you. Just hurry up and get better." Her voice cracked.

A smile tugged at the corners of his mouth. Damn. Even that hurt. "Tuck?"

"I'm here." Tuck's voice sounded rough.

Remaining awake was getting increasingly difficult. "Take care of her," Reaper said, his own voice fading.

"I will," Tuck promised. "Until you're back on your feet. Because you will be back on your feet."

Reaper would have chuckled, but that required more energy than he had. "That an order?"

"You bet."

"Aye, aye," Reaper said then blacked out.

2

One month later

"I'm not ready." Leigha Fields stood in the break room on the first floor of the Orthopedics & Rehabilitation building at Walter Reed Bethesda National Medical Military Center, her heart pounding, her hands sweaty. This case would be her first amputee on her own since she'd completed her training. Yeah, she'd worked with wounded soldiers who had torn ACLs, taken shrapnel to their legs and arms, and had to rebuild the muscles since their injuries. But this was the first amputee. A SEAL who'd lost his arm in a special operation in Afghanistan. "What if I hurt him? What if he refuses to do the exercises I prescribe?"

"You'll do fine. All you have to do is be patient

and remember your training." Eric Shipley, one of the therapists working with wounded warriors, patted her back. "You'll do fine."

"I've never been a patient person," she admitted.

Normally, Leigha went into everything she did without hesitation, full-on, no fear. Her training as a Washington, D.C. cop had prepared her for the worst. Her job on the force had given her the experience with just that. The worst.

Yeah, from cop to physical therapist was a huge change of career. Not one she had chosen for herself. Well, not really.

The daughter of a police officer, she'd never dreamed of being anything else. Both of her brothers had gone into law enforcement. One joined the FBI, the other joined the Alexandria, Virginia Police Department. Her sister had become a nurse and delivered babies in the maternity ward of Bethesda Health. And Leigha had joined the same police department where her father had worked until the day he was shot and killed by a man robbing a liquor store. All over a bottle of whiskey.

Leigha would still be a cop, if she hadn't had a shootout go sideways. Two brothers had ganged up on another man. Their argument drew the attention of a neighbor who'd called 911. Leigha and her partner responded to that call.

When they arrived, the argument escalated.

Leigha and her partner got out of their vehicle, at the same time one of the brothers opened fire, shooting the man in the face. Both brothers ran.

Leigha and her partner gave chase. The brother with the gun ducked behind a trash bin and fired at them.

Her partner went down, clutching his leg, but yelling, "I'm good. Get him!"

Leigha dove to the side, rolled and pushed to her feet, racing after the fleeing men.

The armed man turned and fired his weapon at her. The first shot went wide, the second one hit her in the knee. Leigha hit the ground, her weapon flying free of her hand and skidding across the pavement two feet away. Pain ripped through her leg when she tried putting weight on it, so she dragged, scooted, and pulled herself toward her weapon.

With no one chasing him anymore, the man with the gun stopped running and said something to his brother, then walked toward her, brandishing his gun. "Not so tough now, are you?" As he neared her, he pointed the weapon at her chest. "Well, look here. We got a she-cop. Maybe we could have a little fun with the bitch before we kill her."

Another siren's wail echoed off the brick walls.

The man's brother tugged at his arm. "Shoot her already. We gotta go."

With her gun inches away from her hand, Leigha knew she had only one chance and she had to make it good.

The man pointed the gun at her face.

Pushing hard, Leigha rolled over, grabbed the gun, and lying on her back, shot the man in the chest. The impact at such close quarters flung him backward, knocking his brother on his backside. The dead man's weight on his brother trapped him momentarily. Long enough for Leigha to sit up and take aim at him. "Move, and I'll blow your ass away."

That had been two years ago. One of the brothers died that day. The other was sent to prison as an accessory to the crime.

The gunshot wound to Leigha's knee ended her career on the force. Sure, she could have taken a desk job, but that wasn't an option. She had to be moving. Instead, she'd opted for medical retirement at the ripe old age of twenty-five. This option left her floundering in indecision. She'd never dreamed of doing anything but law enforcement. She wanted to put away thugs who killed people for fun. Baby killers, rapists, and cop killers like the one who'd shot her father.

After six months of knee reconstruction and physical therapy, her physical therapist had encouraged her to go back to school and retrain. Do something with her life, because it wasn't over yet.

Because of the work her therapist had done with her, Leigha could walk practically without a limp and she was jogging a little, though that activity wasn't encouraged on her bionic knee. The elliptical was her friend, helping her to rebuild the strength in her calves and thighs.

Grateful to be back on her feet and almost as good as new, Leigha decided to pursue a career in physical therapy. As part of her curriculum, she'd worked with wounded warriors in Bethesda at the Walter Reed Bethesda National Medical Military Center. She loved working with the military men and women under Eric's mentorship. When she'd been offered a fulltime position on the staff after completion of her coursework and certification, she'd happily accepted.

"Here he comes with his fiancée."

He was tall, but then everyone was tall compared to Leigha. With blond hair hanging longish down past his collar, a sexy five-o'clock shadow at eleven in the morning, and gray-blue eyes, the man was incredibly attractive. Even

Leigha, who'd seen some amazing men pass through the rehab center had to admit he made butterflies flap in her belly. "What's his name?"

"Cory Nipton."

The SEAL frowned as he approached with a pretty, sandy-blond-haired woman. "I understand my normal therapist left."

Eric stepped up to him and smiled. "That's right. But Leigha will be taking over. She's just as capable and will help you through your sessions."

The frown deepened, his brows coming together. "She's just a kid."

A spike of anger rippled up Leigha's spine. But she remembered Eric's warning. Many of the patients had been through a lot. Post-traumatic Stress Disorder (PTSD) was a real issue with depression as a nasty side effect. She reminded herself how she'd felt when her blown-out knee had cost her the only job she'd ever wanted. She'd been sad, angry and depressed. Fighting that range of emotions along with the pain of recovery had been an uphill battle.

Cory Nipton was no different.

She nodded. "The package might be small, but I know how to get the job done." Since she'd come to work with the wounded warriors, she'd learned speaking softly got a lot more cooperation than yelling. But she knew how to be firm and didn't take a speck of guff off anyone.

Having read his file she knew he'd been through several surgeries over the past month, the docs scraping out the shrapnel and shattered bone and cleaning up the dead tissue. Phantom pain had been his enemy during all of that time and still continued to plague him on occasion.

Leigha could work with that. She'd only give him as much as he could handle.

"Can I request a male therapist?" Cory insisted.

His fiancée touched his arm. "Give the woman a chance. She wouldn't be here, if she didn't know what she was doing." She held out a hand. "HI, I'm Delaney O'Connell, Cory's... fiancée."

Leigha gave Delaney a grateful smile. "That's right. So, if you'll come with me, we'll get started."

Cory and his fiancée followed her to a bench near a window that overlooked the well-manicured landscape surrounding Walter Reed. She pointed and said, "Sit."

"You have a lousy bedside manner," Cory grumbled.

"What did you expect? You insulted me." She held out a rubber strap. "Put your injured arm—"

"For the love of Mike, call it what it is. It's a Goddamn stump."

Again, biting on her lip, Leigha forced a smile and a calmness she wasn't feeling, and then nodded. "Okay. Put your arm in the sling. Anchor it around your neck and pull it across your chest. One hundred times."

Cory's eyes widened. "You've got to be kidding me."

Leigh crossed her arms over her chest. "Nope. You're not leaving this room until you've done all one hundred." She stepped back, but didn't leave. "I'm waiting."

"You'll be waiting a long time. I'm not playing stupid games."

"Are you afraid you can't?" she asked, her brows rising.

"Hell, no."

"Then what's your problem?" she asked, her chin lifting.

"He could be in a lot of pain," Delaney said, her mouth drawn tight.

Cory raised his hand, and Delaney didn't say anything else. He took a seat on the bench, eased his stump into the rubber sling, and pulled it across his chest. "This is too easy."

"Stick to the one hundred. When I think you're ready, you can increase that amount." Leigha waited until he started the repetitions, then she turned and walked away to assist another therapist with a double leg amputee. Either he did the exercise or he didn't. Leigha would be back to give him hell if he didn't.

AFTER A MONTH in the hospital with other soldiers in far worse shape than he was, Cory couldn't feel sorry for himself. What was bothering him that day was the fact O'Connell was headed back to the sandbox. He counted off fifty right-arm pulls without talking. The more he did, the harder the action got. Hell, he used to bench press two hundred and fifty pounds. Pulling a rubber strap shouldn't be this hard. Ten more and he breathed hard, sweat popping out on his forehead. He stopped. "What's the use? This won't grow my arm back."

"Cory, you have to do it. I can't go back until I know you'll be okay." Delaney stood beside him.

For Delaney, and to remove the furrow from her pretty brows, he tried again. When he'd moved it only halfway, he let go and growled. "Fuck this!"

The blond physical therapist appeared. "Cory, the only way you'll get better is to fight past the pain, and use those muscles that haven't been used in a month. Now do it."

Her voice was soft but firm, but Cory heard

the steel in it. She wasn't letting him get away with whining or quitting.

"You're new here, aren't you?" Delaney asked.

"Not really. I've been working part-time up until today. Now I'm fulltime and Cory will be working with me." She placed the rubber strap over Cory's arm again and stepped back. "I'll be Cory's physical therapist for the next few weeks."

Cory read between the lines, *Like it or not.* "I don't want a different therapist," Cory groused. "What was wrong with Michaels?"

"He was transferred to San Antonio Medical Center. He's leaving in two weeks." Leigha nodded toward the rubber strap. "Now, give me five more repetitions with the strap."

"I don't have the rest of my arm. Why bother?"

With squinted eyes, she crossed both arms over her chest and leaned close, whispering, "Are you a SEAL or a pansy ass?"

Delaney's brows dipped, but her lips twitched like she couldn't decide whether to bitch at the therapist or laugh.

If Cory had his choice, he wouldn't have minded a little catfight between the two women. Anything to take the attention off of him. The pain ripping through his arm made him grind his teeth, but he'd be damned if he let it show in front of the little fireball of a female therapist.

Leigha raised her brow.

During one of Cory's rest breaks when Leigha had gone off to help another soldier, Delaney touched his shoulder. "Cory, honey, I need to leave. I have to pack and be on the plane in two hours."

"You sure you don't want me to come along to the airport?" Cory looked up. He'd love to go anywhere and get away from the miniature Attila.

Delaney shook her head. "I don't like tearful goodbyes, and I don't want to worry about you getting back to the hospital."

With only one arm. She didn't say it, but Reaper heard it anyway. He captured her hand and held on, as if holding onto the last link to his former life as a SEAL. "I don't know what I would have done without you, O'Connell."

She smiled, and then her gaze flicked to the side.

Even her smile seemed more distant. He could understand. Once you got orders, your mind was a thousand miles ahead. In Delaney's case, it was several thousand miles ahead, across the ocean to the sandbox they'd left behind a month ago. She couldn't stay with him forever, playing nursemaid. She had a military career.

Anger and pain seared through him. What the hell kind of life would he have post-military?

All he knew were tactics and shooting. Hell, now he couldn't even shoot. His trigger finger and entire arm were gone.

A wave of anger and depression washed over his thoughts. He fought to keep it from showing in his face. O'Connell didn't need to leave feeling sorry for him. She needed a clear head and conscience to see her through the tough jobs she had ahead. The woman was still working to prove herself with the 160th Night Stalkers. A month on leave wasn't helping, and Reaper had been selfish to want her to stay. He stood and faced her. If he was fair, he'd tell her to forget their engagement. Go. Find a whole man who can give you what you deserve. Love, an exciting life, and the ability to hug you with both arms.

For a long moment, O'Connell stared up into his eyes, her gaze searching his. Then she leaned up on her toes and kissed him.

She linked her hands behind his head and gave him the first real kiss he'd gotten. He cupped the back of her neck and thrust his tongue past his lips to tangle with hers. Before he'd lost his arm...before O'Connell, he'd been a player, flirting with women and kissing indiscriminately. He considered himself a good kisser. But something wasn't right in the kiss he shared now with O'Connell. Sure she'd pecked his lips, kissed his forehead, and let him kiss hers, but they'd never really shared a let's-get-naked-and-fuck kiss.

"Eh-hem. Want me to come back later?" Leigha stood behind Reaper with her brows raised.

O'Connell straightened, her cheeks burning. "No. I was just leaving."

"Take your time. I'm here all day." She winked at Reaper and performed a perky about-face.

O'Connell chuckled. "I think you've met your match in that one."

"Yeah." Reaper frowned, his gaze following the woman across the floor. Then he turned to O'Connell. "Promise me you'll Skype when you can."

"I'll try." She slipped her purse strap onto her shoulder. "With the time difference, I'm not sure how often I can."

"And tell Tuck I'm okay. He's probably blaming himself." Reaper stared down at his arm. "He shouldn't. I don't."

"I'll let him know." O'Connell hesitated. "Cory?"

"Yeah, babe?" He still held her hand, weaving his fingers through hers.

She swallowed hard and cleared her throat. "You realize that was our first real kiss."

"I know." He smiled. "I'm just sad it wasn't before..." He shrugged. "You know."

"Before you lost your arm?"

Reaper winced. O'Connell called it as it was.

"That doesn't matter," she said.

"Does to me. It might have been better."

"The kiss?"

"Yeah."

"You didn't feel anything, either?" she asked.

Reaper's brows furrowed. "Is that what you think?" He pulled her into his one-armed embrace and kissed the top of her head. "Of course I did."

O'Connell's brows wrinkled, and she bit on her bottom.

"Wait," Reaper said, a single word echoing in his thoughts. His chest tightened.

Pressing her lips tight, she glanced up at him.

Reaper set her at arm's length, his frown deepening. "Either? Are you telling me you didn't feel it?"

She hesitated, glanced to a far corner and then said, in a flat tone, "I wanted to."

He tipped up her chin and stared into her blue eyes, his gut clenching. This was O'Connell, his best friend. "I thought you loved me."

She touched his arm. "I do. I'm just not sure it's the kind of love you need."

"O'Connell, I've loved you from the first time

you spilled popcorn on the couch in our apartment at Little Creek."

She smiled through tear-filled eyes. "Tuck was mad. He missed a pass by the Miami Dolphins when they played the New England Patriots."

Tuck had been mad. The couch was brand new, never initiated with food or drink. "He got over it. Especially when you started picking up all the popcorn in his lap. Seems to me he forgot all about the game." Reaper grinned. "For a while there, I thought you two would get together."

Eyes widening, O'Connell opened her mouth.

Before she could say anything, Reaper continued. "But when he didn't make a move, I figured I had a shot. So, you didn't feel anything when we kissed?" He shook his head. "Then I'm not giving my best." He winked. "I used to have a reputation with the women, until I met you. I had a knack for flirting." His chest puffed out.

"Why did you stop flirting?"

All the air left his lungs, and he sagged. "What's it matter? I got my girl. Why should I flirt?"

"Cory, you can't wait around for me. What if I don't come back?"

His chest pinched. Even if he hadn't felt anything with their kiss, he still loved her and

Tuck. They were his family. "You're too damned good a helicopter pilot to bite the big one in the sandbox. You'll be back."

"But—"

"I don't want to hear it. One of us has to carry on the tradition of duty, honor, and country."

Searching his face, she pressed a finger to his lips. "Promise me this."

He captured the finger and kissed the tip. "Anything."

"Keep your options open."

He frowned. "I love you, O'Connell. I don't want anything else."

"Promise me," she insisted, narrowing her gaze.

He didn't want anyone else. O'Connell was tough, smart, and everything he could want in a wife. "I'll think about it." Again, O'Connell appeared to want to say more but bit her lip again instead.

Finally, she said, "Play nice with your therapist and be strong."

"I have to be. We're getting married when you get back." He drew her close with his good arm and crushed her lips with his, hoping the second real kiss had more spark than the first.

When he broke off the kiss, he couldn't deny the distinct feeling he was kissing a friend, not a lover.

O'Connell ducked her head and hurried away.

Reaper let his gaze follow her until she disappeared. Was he wrong to want her as his wife? After the two kisses, he found himself questioning everything about their relationship. But he'd proposed, and she'd accepted. He couldn't go back on his word. At the same time, he couldn't hold her to her promise when he'd forced an answer during a traumatic moment and he wasn't even sure he'd ever find another job. How would he contribute to their marriage?

He wasn't the kind of man who'd live off his wife's income. Reaper had a lot of thinking to do. But within moments, the golden-haired Attila descended, and put him back to work.

Where had such a petite and pretty young woman learned to be so damned bossy? Reaper didn't know, but by the end of his sessions together, he'd find out. Maybe she'd mellow by then. All he knew was at that moment, with the pain shooting through his arm, he hated her with a passion, he hated that he'd lost his limb and the only job he'd ever loved, and he hated that he would probably lose O'Connell and Tuck, the truest friends he'd ever known.

3

A s Leigha drove to the rehab center at the end of the week, she went over all the progress she'd made with each patient. She'd worked with a number of soldiers with varying degrees of disabilities—from those with injuries that would see full recovery to those who had to learn how to deal with a new way of life. Thankfully, most had family by their side, giving them the love and support they desperately needed at this critical juncture in their lives.

The one patient who stood out the most was the Navy SEAL, Cory Nipton, or Reaper as he'd asked her repeatedly to call him. After his fiancée left on Monday, he'd buckled down about going through the paces she put him through, working so hard, he'd exceeded her physical expectations. But a hollowness was in his eyes, and a sense of someone lost in a world he knew nothing about that haunted her each night.

The man had dedicated his life to being a SEAL. He couldn't conceive of a life without the camaraderie of his teammates. The more Leigha thought about him, the more she knew she had to do something to shake him out of his funk. As soon as she reported in for work, she shifted her schedule to place him at the end of the day then made a few calls and reservations. Maybe her surprise would give him the incentive to re-engage in life.

When she'd been at her lowest after her injury and subsequent medical retirement from the force, she'd been in a similar state of mind. Then her brother on the Alexandria police force had shown up at her apartment, loaded her in his truck, and taken her to where Leigha would be taking Reaper. That day had sparked life in her otherwise-dead existence. She hoped her plan had the same effect on Reaper.

Excitement built as the day went by. Several times she thought she saw him pass through the center, but when she had the time to look around, he wasn't there. Until four o'clock rolled around.

Reaper walked in, tall, broad-shouldered, his tattoos peeking out from under his T-shirt in bold black. His expression was withdrawn, his eyes hollow.

A smile formed on her lips, and for the first time in a long time, butterflies fluttered against the inside lining of her belly. "Hey, sunshine, why so glum?"

"I'm not glum," he said, his tone flat, humorless.

"Uh-huh. I could tell." She put him to work on his repetitions, keeping the routine light. She wanted him to have enough energy for later.

As if on automatic, Reaper performed the strength exercises without comment, staring into the distance, not focusing on anything or anyone.

Yeah, he needed something different. The sterile environment of the hospital was getting to him. Or worse, it was giving him too much of a refuge and preventing him from venturing out into the world where people would point and stare at the man with one arm.

Well, he'd have to get over that. Her planned surprise might shock him, but in the long run, it might help him to learn how to adjust to being left-handed. New to the rehab center, Leigha was almost certain what she was about to do wasn't sanctioned and might just be against the rules, but something drove her to bend them a little. Anything to get Reaper to enter and embrace his new life.

After thirty minutes, the man hadn't even broken a sweat. It was time for Leigha to clock out and head home. Seeing Reaper start to leave, she touched his injured arm. "Are you up for a field trip?"

He stopped and stared at the hand resting on his stump, his eyes narrowing. "What are you talking about?"

"Do you feel like blowing this joint and breathing some fresh air?"

He shifted his gaze to her face. "You realize I'm an engaged man?"

She shrugged. "I'm not asking you out on a date. I'm asking if you want to get out of here for a little R&R. You've worked hard all this week, and I have a surprise planned that might cheer you up."

His brows lowered. "I don't need cheering, and I don't need fresh air."

She stared, her lips firming into a straight line. "Look. I could use some company. You don't have anyone to hang out with, so what's it going to hurt? Unless you're afraid to step outside this hospital. Afraid to face the world."

"Why should I care? Once I leave here, I have nowhere to go. No job. No family. Why should I care about going for a joy ride with my therapist? It's dumb. A waste of time for me, and definitely a waste of time for you." He started to move past her.

Again, she placed a hand on his arm, remembering Eric's advice to be patient. But her patience was waning. "You should care because you have a lovely fiancée who would be appalled to see the man she loves moping and feeling sorry for himself, when he should be exploring his options and building a new life that could include her."

She let go of his arm and stepped back. "Wallow in your self-pity. That's your choice. I'm going for a ride. If you want to come with me, meet me out in the parking lot. I drive a black Jeep Wrangler with a hard top. I'm leaving in ten minutes." She turned and walked away—disappointed, sad and, most of all, angry. The man was on a downward spiral. If he didn't pull himself out, he'd crash and burn. Suicide rates among veterans were shockingly high. Leigha was damned if he took his own life on her watch.

REAPER STOMPED HALFWAY BACK to his room before he realized Leigha had been right. From the moment he'd come to the hospital in Bethesda, he'd been angry, stubborn, despondent, and less than cooperative. For the past week,

Leigha had been extremely patient and firm, driving him in the direction of recovery. He'd worked hard, but his heart wasn't in regime. What would happen to him when he was released? He had nowhere to go. No job waiting and what could he do? Sitting behind a desk would absolutely suck the life out of him. Working outdoors usually required two arms and two hands.

The occupational therapist had been working to reteach him out to write, brush his teeth, and comb his hair. When he'd lost his right arm, he'd practically lost his entire ability to function. He resented fumbling with his left hand. He looked like a kindergarten kid, holding a pen and no matter how hard he tried, he couldn't hold his toothbrush properly when he brushed his teeth. Buttoning buttons, putting on socks...hell, zipping his fly... were all challenges because he'd never done them with his left hand.

Why would he go out in public where people would laugh when he lifted his fork to his mouth and half of the contents fell into his lap?

He checked the watch on his left wrist. Eight minutes had passed since Leigha left him. In two more minutes, she'd drive out of the parking lot.

So?

He turned, his feet carrying him toward the exit, as if they were in control. As he pushed through the exit door, he cursed. This was ridiculous. Why was he headed for the parking lot when he had no intention of going with the physical therapist?

Blinking against the sunlight, he scanned the rows of vehicles. So many were black SUVs. She could have left already. Reaper told himself he didn't care. He was about to turn and reenter the building when a black Jeep Wrangler pulled up to the curb, and the window slid down.

Leigha leaned across the console and called out, "Get in."

For a second, he hesitated.

"Or don't." She raised the window and shifted into drive.

Reaper lunged for the handle, fumbled with his left hand, yanked open the door, and dropped into the passenger seat.

Leigha smiled at him but didn't say a word. She pressed her foot to the accelerator, drove out of the parking lot, and away from the hospital.

After a glance around, Reaper settled back in his seat, a frown pinching his brow, not sure he'd done the right thing, but committed now, whether he liked it or not. "Where are we going?"

"You'll see," she said in a singsong voice.

"You can stop being so damned cheerful."

"And you can stop biting my head off." She shot him a wide grin. "Come on. The sun is shining—"

"It's cloudy."

"The birds are singing—"

"Can't hear them over the roar of traffic."

"And you're out of the hospital," she ended, her tone flat.

Reaper snorted. "One out of three isn't bad."

"Now you're being optimistic." Her smile was back.

"Don't get used to it." Reaper glanced out the window, for the first time taking note of his surroundings. Leigha was right. In between drifting white clouds, blue sky and sunshine peeked through. The grass and trees were green, unlike the drab tans and brown of the dessert.

He had spent far too much time inside. "How long until we get there?"

"Fifteen minutes, depending on traffic."

Reaper sat silent for a while, then glanced at Leigha. "So, what's your story?"

Her lips pulled up on the side. "I don't have a story."

"Everyone has a story."

She shrugged. "What's yours?"

Regretting starting the conversation, he stared out the front windshield, the pain in his chest pressing hard against his heart. But he'd started it. "Orphaned at fourteen, in foster care until I finished high school." He fought the clenching of his jaw to finish. "Joined the navy, became a SEAL, stepped on a trip wire, kicked out of the service, the end." He turned to her. "Your turn."

She bit her lip, her fingers tightening on the steering wheel until her knuckles turned white. For a long time she maneuvered through traffic without speaking.

About the time Reaper thought she wouldn't respond, he heard her speak. "Large family of cops, majored in criminology in college, worked for D.C. police department, got shot, and like you, medically retired. Retrained and now I'm a physical therapist."

He stared, trying to imagine her in uniform. "They let you be a police officer?"

"Let?" Her brows dipped. "I was a damned good one."

Reaper discovered he liked the way Leigha's blue eyes sparkled when she was angry. A smile tugged at the corners of his lips. For the first time in a long time, he relaxed. "A cop, huh?" He shook his head. "Can't see it." In his mind, at best, she was a meter maid, writing tickets to people who parked in the wrong place.

She didn't rise to his bait, but her lips thinned.

"Ever shoot someone?" he asked. He'd done his share. As a team sniper, he'd shot a lot of people, many of which he'd never even seen their faces.

Again, she didn't respond for a long time. Finally, she said, "I did."

All joking aside, he could sense telling him that bit of information had taken a lot, indicating it had been a traumatic experience. "What happened?"

"The perp shot a man then shot me. Then he and his brother doubled back to finish the job, and I shot him."

"Was he the only one?"

"After four years on the force, in one of the most crime-ridden cities in the country, my first and last was that man."

"And the brother?"

"Locked up."

"For how long?"

She shrugged. At the sentencing, LeVon's brother Jamal Clayton glared her way as the judge sentenced him. "Ten years. He was eighteen. They went easy on him since he didn't pull the trigger."

Reaper wasn't as familiar with the D.C. legal system or the prisons on the east coast. But he was familiar with the gang warfare in L.A. Avenging a brother's death was expected. "How many years ago was that?"

"Two and a half."

"When is he eligible for parole?"

"I'm not sure."

"You shot his brother. Aren't you afraid he'll get out and come after you?"

Leigha waved a hand. "He was just a kid. I'm not on the force anymore."

"A thug who's been in the system, around men who have done worse crimes, comes out even harder than he went in."

"I have my conceal carry license." Her brothers had insisted she get one. She hadn't argued. A woman couldn't be too careful.

"Check on his parole."

"All right, already. I'll check. In the meantime, we're here." She pulled into a parking lot.

Reaper had been so caught up in the discussion about her shooting he hadn't paid much attention to where they were. When he glanced up at the huge sign hanging across the front of a huge steel building, he felt a lead weight settle in the pit of his belly.

Mid-Atlantic Indoor Range.

"What the fuck?" Reaper shook his head. "Take me back. You have to be out of your fucking mind."

Leigha pulled the keys from the ignition, got out, rounded to his side, and opened his door.

He refused to get out.

She leaned in. "You were a sniper, right?"

The cotton candy scent of her perfume wrapped around him. "*Was* is the operative word. That part of my life is gone." He waved his stump. "Gone with my right arm and hand."

"Look, big guy, you have another hand, another arm. In case you didn't notice, some of the other wounded warriors have neither and would give anything to have what you have." She pointed to the ground. "Get out of the car and man up. You've been walking around for the past month like a dead man."

"I might as well be dead," he muttered, staring at the tops of his shoes.

"Bullshit. Tonight, we begin the reincarnation of Cory Nipton. On your feet, soldier."

Reaper glared into her blue eyes, hating her pretty face and the cleavage he could see so well with her leaning over him. Hated that, at that moment, he wanted to punch her in the face as much as he wanted to kiss her until she gasped for breath. "I'm not a soldier."

"Even more reason for you to prove you're a man. Let's go." She turned and marched into the building, her petite body incongruous with her military bearing.

He had two choices. Sit in the hot vehicle or follow her into the range. Telling himself he'd rather wait where the space was air-conditioned, he got out, locked the Jeep, and entered the indoor range.

Inside the scent of cleaning oil and gunpowder filled his nostrils and bought on such a heavy feeling of nostalgia, he almost turned and walked back out. God, he missed his team. He missed training with them and missed going out on missions with them. For the first month, he worried about who was covering Tuck's six and what Big Bird, Fish, Gator, and Nacho were up to. Had they gone back into the hills to find the Taliban leader they'd sought when they'd walked into the trap where Reaper had tripped the explosion?

He had refused to Skype with his friends. Especially Tuck. Reaper was afraid he'd break down when he saw Tuck, still in the desert, still a part of the team. But damn, maybe it was time he did. Tuck and the other members of his team were like brothers. Hell, they were closer than brothers. They'd been to hell and back together. That counted more than blood.

When he got back to his room, he'd power up the laptop O'Connell had given him and contact Tuck. Over a month had passed. He could do it. *Should* do it. He needed to know how they were.

Leigha stood at the counter, turning a pistol over in her hand. "Yes, this one will do for me."

"What about him?" the man behind the

counter asked.

"You'll have to ask him?" Leigha turned to Reaper. "Nine millimeter Berretta or an HK 40 like I have?"

"Neither. I'll just watch."

"Wrong." Leigha turned to the man. "Nine millimeter Berretta and forty rounds."

Irritation at her attitude forced Reaper forward. "Sig-Sauer P226."

"Now you're talking. We just got two in. Brand new." He turned to a locked cabinet behind him and extracted the nine-millimeter handgun. "It'll be perfect for you because of the ambidextrous magazine release and fifteen-round capacity. Have to reload less often."

"I know its capabilities," Reaper cut in. He'd carried one on him into hostile territory along with his M4A1 with the SOPMOD upgrade. Whatever he wanted, he'd gotten.

The man laid the weapon on the counter, rather than handing it to Reaper.

Reaper clenched his teeth and reached for the grip, his left hand fumbling, before he finally raised it and held it in his palm. The weapon felt odd in his left hand. But strangely familiar. He and his teammates had naturally practiced firing with their dominant hands, as well as their non-dominant hands. He'd done all right. Not nearly as accurate as he'd been with his right hand.

Leigha and Reaper signed forms, were issued eye and ear protection, and assigned booth numbers next to each other. They gathered targets, weapons and the ammunition, and then passed through a door into the large indoor range. Several men and one woman occupied booths and were firing downrange.

Once in their booths, Leigh and Reaper slipped on their eye and ear protection. The glasses were scuffed and difficult to see through. The fact frustrated Reaper who was used to only the best equipment. But then it didn't matter. He wouldn't shoot worth a crap anyway.

Loading bullets into the magazine proved to be more difficult than firing the weapon. After trying to hold the magazine with his stump or between his knees, he figured out how to hold it at the very end with his last two fingers and press the rounds in with his thumb. Leigha was already firing by the time he had fifteen rounds in the magazine and shoved it into the P226. He fumbled with the target, eventually managing to clip it to the line, and sent it downrange.

With his target in position, he raised the P226 and sighted down the barrel. His hand shook as he squeezed off a round. The shot went wide, missing the target altogether. Reaper glanced at Leigha's target and swallowed a groan.

She had a tight pattern of bullet holes in the

area of the heart and another in the silhouette of the head. The woman was an amazing shot. A complete dichotomy from the cute, petite blond image she portrayed.

He grinned and focused on his own target, concentrated on keeping his hand steady and fired. This time, not only did he hit the target, he hit the silhouette in the right shoulder. He adjusted his aim and fired again, hitting dead center in what would be a man's chest. The more he fired, the closer his shots grouped. By the time he emptied the magazine, he had a tight shot group centered on the heart.

He brought forward his target.

Leigha entered his booth and nodded. She didn't smile and didn't patronize him, just nodded. Then she left him alone with the parting words. "Do it again."

Reaper left the range a different man from the one who hadn't wanted to enter in the first place.

He wouldn't admit the truth out loud, but Leigha had been right. He had to accept he wouldn't ever return to being a SEAL, and find new purpose in his life. What that was he didn't know, but he'd proved one thing tonight—he wasn't done.

4

Street lights blinked on as darkness cloaked the city. Leigha drove back to Reaper's place, a smile on her face and an odd ache in her heart. She could tell by the confidence with which Reaper walked out of the indoor range, he was beginning to learn something about his new self. He could do whatever he set his mind to.

The problem she had with his new confidence was that the combination of a hot body, confidence, and a sexy grin had turned her stomach upside down every time he aimed the attitude her way. She could see the man he'd once been and was becoming again. His change made her chest tight and her core hot. How long since she'd been with a man? So long her batteries on her vibrator had been replaced twice.

She hadn't dated since her accident. Really, since well before her accident. As a cop, she tended to intimidate men. Yeah, she wasn't afraid to speak her mind and shoot a perp, if the situation called for it. Deep inside, she was still a woman with emotions and feelings. Like anyone, she wanted someone in her life to love and hold her at night.

The traffic wasn't particularly horrible between the shooting range and the rehab center. Reaper sat silent in the seat beside her, seemingly lost in his thoughts.

At least the silence was comfortable, one Leigha was happy to accommodate. She had her own thinking to do.

Reaper was her patient. She had to remind herself of this fact often. The repercussions of having anything beyond a professional relationship would be too much to deal with at this time in her life. It could cost her the job she'd just been offered. Not that she would allow herself to become too involved in his life. Once he was through with his therapy, he'd move on. No need would exist for them to come into contact with each other again.

As she approached a turn, she put on her blinker, indicating her direction. Before she even started turning, her Jeep slammed forward. The seatbelt tightened, saving her face from hitting the steering wheel.

"What the fuck!" Reaper shouted beside her. He twisted in his seat and glanced behind them. "He's going to hit us again," Reaper warned.

At first, Leigha didn't understand what was happening. She held her foot on the brake, but her Jeep slammed forward again. Her gaze shifted to the rearview mirror, but all she could see were headlights coming at her for a third hit. Instinct and her police training kicked in and she jammed her foot on the accelerator, shooting ahead.

The vehicle slammed into her bumper and pushed her forward even faster.

Leigha gripped the steering wheel and desperately dodged the cars parked along the side of the street. The traffic light ahead blinked yellow then red, and vehicles pulled through the intersection.

"Turn right!" Reaper yelled, his hand braced on the dashboard.

Leigha didn't hesitate. She jerked the wheel to the right and hit the accelerator. The car behind continued forward, pushing the rear of her car into a spin. Leigha kept her cool, let off the gas, and straightened the Jeep when the vehicle behind her sped past.

"That's right. You've got it now."

She shot a brief glance at the other vehicle.

Brake lights glared red. Ahead, the attacking vehicle skidded to a stop and white reverse lights flashed on.

"He's coming back. Go, go, go!" Reaper shouted.

Heart racing, Leigha slammed her foot to the accelerator. The Jeep shot forward. Barely slowing at stop signs and stop lights, she drove on, twisting and turning through the city streets, her gaze again and again shifting from the road to the rearview mirror. When she felt they'd lost their tail, she slowed, pulled to a stop at a well-lit convenience store, and took a deep breath for the first time in what had to have been an hour, but in fact was only five minutes.

"What the hell was that all about?" Reaper asked.

"I don't know." Leigha grabbed her cell phone and called 911. "You didn't happen to get a make or model on the vehicle, did you?"

Reaper shook his head. "It happened too fast."

Moments later, a police car pulled up beside them in the parking lot. Leigha reported the incident, but she didn't have much to go on. "The vehicle appeared to be a dark sedan. I'm not even certain if it had two or four doors. Whatever it was, it will have a smashed front end from ramming the back of my Jeep." She stood at the back of her vehicle, staring at the crushed bumper and tailgate, angry someone had the balls to ram her, saddened her pretty Jeep was a mess, but thankful she and Reaper hadn't been injured in the incident.

Even after over two years away from the police force, she felt weird being on the other side of the uniform.

The policeman took the information, handed her a business card, and left.

Leigha glanced at Reaper. "You sure you're all right?"

He nodded, his brows furrowed, and he cupped her face with his hand, brushing his thumb across her cheek. "I'm fine. I'm more worried about you."

He stared at her with those gray eyes, darkened with concern. Her heart thudded against her ribs and her pulse rocketed through her veins. This time, due to the way Reaper looked at her, not because of the near disaster caused by a hit-and-run driver. "I'm fine," she said. "Just a little shaken."

She was shaking. Her knees threatened to buckle, and she had the intense desire to kiss the sexy SEAL.

His hand slipped down to her shoulder, and

he pulled her against him. "I have to admit, for a moment, I had a flashback to the explosion that earned me a one-way ticket out of Afghanistan."

"Oh, Reaper." She raised her hand to his face.

He caught it and pressed his lips to her fingertips. "I don't need your pity."

Her fingers tingled where his lips had been. "Not pity. Empathy." She lifted her chin. "Have I ever been soft on you, Nipton?" His full lips spread in a wide grin that made Leigha's insides melt.

"Never. I had drill sergeants in BUD/s training who were kinder and gentler."

Before she leaned up and embarrassed herself by kissing a patient, an engaged one at that, Leigha backed away, dropping her hands to her sides. "Good. Nice to know I'm effective. Get in. I'll take you back to your place." She climbed in and waited for him to slide into the passenger seat.

On the way back to his place, Reaper commented, "Something stinks out of that whole incident. Why would someone ram into you?"

After Leigha pushed her thoughts of kissing Reaper to the back of her mind, she'd been asking herself the same question. "It could have been a random attack."

Reaper shook his head. "One hit is an accident. The second and third hits were deliberate. The question is why."

"Gang initiation?" She suggested. "I'll bet the vehicle was stolen, and the police find it abandoned on some street by morning. Crap like that happened all the time in D.C. Gang initiation."

"Yeah, but we're not in D.C."

"Gangs are found all over the country."

Reaper turned to her. "Humor me and make some calls to your old contacts. Find out if any of the people you sent to jail were released recently."

She nodded, already on board with the idea. "Deal."

"What kind of security do you have at your place?"

"I live in a gated apartment complex."

"What about your apartment? Any security cameras? Do you have an alarm system on your doors and windows?"

She shot him a frown. "No."

"You might want to get them."

"Thanks for your concern. But I'm not made of money."

"Then get a dog. A big one. A German Shepherd."

She laughed. "Calm down. I'll be all right. I told you, I have a gun."

"On you?" He angled his head and scanned her from head to toe.

"In my purse."

"You need to carry it on your body."

"I appreciate your concern, but I can take care of myself."

He sat back in his seat, the frown still furrowing his brow. "I'd feel better if you stayed with someone else tonight. You said you have brothers?"

"I do. But they live too far. I have work in the morning." She touched his arm. "I'll be okay."

"I'd feel better if someone stayed with you."

"Are you volunteering?" she asked before she thought the situation through.

"Yes." His chin dipped in a curt nod.

"Sorry. I can't have a patient staying at my place. Doing that would be breaking all the rules."

"You're a therapist, not a doctor."

"It's part of my contract with the rehab center."

"I won't tell, if you won't."

"But I'll know."

"It can be our secret for tonight and tomorrow. Then you can make it right and transfer me to another therapist."

"No." The conversation had gone on long enough. Leigha pulled up in front of his quarters.

"I'll see you tomorrow. If you want a new therapist then, you have that right, and I'll make it happen. Until then, I'll be just fine."

Reaper turned in his seat, his gaze intense. "Call me and let me know you got back to your apartment okay."

"Okay," Leigha conceded. "I'll call."

He gave her his number. She punched in the numbers and let the call connect so that he'd have hers. "Now, can I go? I have a full day tomorrow. I need sleep."

Reaper leaned across the console and pressed his lips to hers. "I've wanted to do that all evening. If it breaks the rules, sue me." Then he did it again, this time cupping the back of her head and pressing his mouth to hers, skimming the seam of her lips with his tongue.

Too surprised to protest, Leigha opened to him and he slipped inside, his tongue sliding along hers, in a long, steady glide. He tasted of mint and made her insides burn with a burgeoning desire.

Despite all her protestations of therapist/patient relations, she raised her hand to his face and melted into the kiss. Yes, his lips were as sensual as they appeared and his tongue was doing crazy things to her self-control. She could imagine how amazing having the hardened tips of her nipples licked, one at a time, would feel.

When he broke the kiss, his nostrils flaring, he brushed his thumb across her mouth. "Get me a new therapist." Then he climbed out of the Jeep, poking his head back in the door. "I mean it. Call me when you get to your apartment."

His voice, low and gravelly, melted her all the way to her core. She nodded, unable to form a single coherent word or thought. Out of rote memory, she shifted into drive and pulled away from the curb. When she glanced in her rearview mirror, she spotted Reaper standing where she'd left him.

Every last bit of her self-control was needed to keep driving when all she wanted to do was turn around, beg him to get in and come back to her apartment, and make crazy, sweet love with her through the night. Yeah. She would fail the cardinal rule of a fulltime physical therapist. *Don't fall for your patient.*

AFTER LEIGHA DISAPPEARED out of sight, Reaper hurried to his room, booted up his computer, and searched the internet for Brotherhood Protectors, a fairly new organization established by an old friend from BUD/s training, Hank "Montana" Patterson. He might have connections who could do some digging.

An answering machine picked up on the second ring.

"This is the Brotherhood Protectors. Leave a message, and we'll get back to you during regular office hours. If this is an emergency, dial..."

Reaper committed the emergency number to memory, ended the call, and dialed it.

"Hank speaking."

"Hank, Cory Nipton, you might remember me from BUD/s."

"Reaper! I sure as hell do. Good to hear from you. Where are you these days?"

Reaper filled him in on all that had happened in succinct, emotionless sentences including the attack that evening.

Hank listened without commenting until Reaper was done. "I'm sorry to hear about your loss. What is it you want me to do? I currently have all my guys out on assignment. I could be there myself in three hours, though. I'm in Chicago, headed your way. I have to be in Alexandria tomorrow, anyway."

"No. Like Leigha said, this could have been a random attack. Leigha was a cop in D.C. Do you have any connections who could dig into her arrest and sentencing record and find out if any of her jailbirds are up for or have been paroled who might have a bone to pick?"

Hank paused. "I'll get my computer guy on it. Is this number a good one to reach you at?"

"It is."

"Good. When I'm done with my meeting in Alexandria, I'd like to swing your way. If I have any news, I can pass it on then. Otherwise, I'd enjoy catching up on old times."

"You're on. Call me when you're near. I'm not going anywhere." Reaper ended the call, realizing how true his parting comment was. Once he was through therapy, then what? He supposed he would find a job. Doing what, he hadn't a clue. His entire life had been focused on a career in the navy. Suddenly thrust into the civilian world, he didn't know here to start.

Well, he'd just have to, what was it Leigha had told him? Man up.

A smile tugged his lips at the image of Leigha after he'd kissed her. Her blue eyes had been wide, her lips slightly swollen, and her blond hair curling around her chin. In some ways, she reminded him of O'Connell—her strength, determination, and ability to stand up to men twice her size.

In other ways, she was completely different. The kiss had spark. An entire electrical current that zipped throughout his body, culminating in his groin. Even now his jeans were tight, making it difficult to walk without adjusting.

When he'd kissed O'Connell before she left, he hadn't felt that spark. He'd brushed it off as a first kiss that would get better in subsequent kisses.

O'Connell.

To be fair to her, he should contact her and confess what he'd done.

Guilt overwhelmed him. He was engaged to O'Connell, and he'd kissed another woman. After all the time she'd spent with him through his surgeries and recovery, he repaid her by cheating. He tapped his keyboard, bringing up the video chat application he and O'Connell used to communicate. The time would be early morning in Afghanistan. Hopefully she'd be awake, getting ready to go for a run.

After several rings, her image appeared, her sandy blond hair rumpled like she'd just gotten out of the rack. "Reaper?"

"Hey. Did I wake you?"

She rubbed her eyes and yawned. "Yeah. But I needed to get up anyway. How are you feeling? Are you getting along with your new therapist?"

"Sure." That twinge of guilt almost tied his tongue. "I have a question for you."

She pushed her hair out of her face and blinked several times before saying, "Shoot."

"When we kissed goodbye..."

Her eyes flared and her face tightened. "What about it?"

"How did it make you feel?"

She looked away from the screen. "You video chat me at six in the morning to ask how I felt about a kiss?" Her eyes narrowed, and she stared at the screen. "Are you sure you're okay?"

"I'm fine. Never better and thinking more clearly than I have in a long time." He sighed. "Did you feel a spark?"

"A spark?" She shook her head. "I don't know what you mean."

"You know, like chemistry when our lips met." He waved his hand, struggling for the right words and not finding them. "I sound like a fucking idiot." He stared back at her and blurted, "O'Connell, let's cut to the chase. Did you *feel* anything when we kissed?"

She stared at him for a long moment without moving.

Reaper thought the video feed had frozen and reached to hit the refresh key.

But then O'Connell bit her lip, her face tensed, and she said, "Of course, I did."

He looked into the face of one of the best friends he'd ever had and forced a smile. "Okay then."

"Is that why you called me?" she asked.

"That, and I was thinking about you and

wanted to see your face." He wasn't lying. No matter how confused he might be, he would always love O'Connell.

But he couldn't make himself tell her that he'd kissed another woman. Not while she was deployed. He didn't want to guess how that would impact her ability to concentrate when she flew missions. She needed all her focus to be on the job she performed. He would be selfish if he confessed his infidelity when what she needed was to know everything was okay back home. Time enough for him to share what he'd done. In the meantime, he wouldn't repeat his transgression with the pretty little therapist.

He owed it to O'Connell, his fiancée to be true. When she got back...then maybe he'd tell her...until then, he would behave himself. No more kissing the therapist.

As he lay in his bed, sleep refused to come right away. An image of Leigha's face plagued him. Her freshly kissed lips, almost begging for another. *Fuck*. What kind of new hell was this?

5

Leigha spent that night with her H&K .40 caliber pistol beneath her pillow, loaded, with the safety locked. By morning, she was kicking herself for letting talk of paroled offenders scare her into a sleepless night of tossing and turning.

She rose before her alarm, dressed, and made a large cup of coffee to jolt her brain into gear. Any sleep she'd actually gotten had been plagued with dreams of kissing Reaper. Not only kissing him, but lying naked in bed beside him, running her hands over his tattooed chest, down his ripped abs, and over his...

Leigha slammed her coffee mug on the table, hot liquid spilling over the edge onto her hand. "Damn it." This was not happening. Her first real therapy case on her own, and she was falling for her patient. If only he hadn't crossed the line and kissed her, she might have resisted her attraction, pushing it to the back of her mind while she worked with him in her sessions. But now...Holy hell, she'd tasted the forbidden fruit and there was no wiping it from her mind.

As she left her apartment, she patted her purse with her pistol tucked inside and made a thorough perusal of the parking lot before she walked to her Jeep. One circle around her poor, damaged Jeep reassured her nothing had been tampered with since the incident the night before. By the time she slid behind the wheel and locked the doors, she was convinced she was overreacting to a random act of thuggery.

Morning rush hour was particularly insane on her way to work, with people pulling out in front of her vehicle and nearly sideswiping her. She reached the rehab center with no incident, but her nerves were frayed and her lack of sleep topped with a heavy dose of caffeine weren't helping.

"You look like hell," Eric greeted her in the break room.

"Thanks," she snarled. "I love you, too."

"What's got your scrubs in a twist?"

"Nothing." *Everything. One SEAL in particular.*

Eric checked the schedule. "You have a pretty

full day, but one of your guys cancelled. Mind if I give you one of mine?"

"I don't mind. Who cancelled?"

"Nipton."

Her heart skipped several beats and then raced on. "Oh, yeah?"

"Yeah. Called first thing this morning and said he had an appointment he couldn't miss at the same time this afternoon."

Perhaps he'd had an attack of guilt. After all, he had a fiancée deployed to Afghanistan.

"About Nipton—"

"Did you hear, Pendley handed in his resignation? He's taken a job in Richmond as head of a small physical therapy clinic. That's going to leave us really shorthanded until we can hire in a couple more therapists." Eric glanced up. "What about Nipton?"

"Nothing." She checked her schedule and headed out onto the floor in search of her first patient. She couldn't pass Reaper to anyone else when the staff were already shorthanded. Besides, what excuse would she give? *I kissed a patient and want to go to bed with him. Is there a problem?*

Her career as a therapist would be over practically before it got started. She would have failed at two careers, and she hadn't even hit thirty. No. She had to get a grip on her feelings, squelch her desire, and keep marching. Changing careers now wasn't an option, and her stint here was too short to job hop to another clinic. She didn't have enough experience on her resume to attract any other offers.

As she worked through the day, she wondered what *appointment* Reaper had that was so important he couldn't complete his session. Or if there really was an appointment. At lunch, she got on the phone with Caitlynn Tate, the prosecuting attorney she'd dealt with during her stint as an officer of the DCPD.

Her secretary patched the call through.

"Officer Fields, what can I do for you?" Caitlynn answered.

"First off, I'm not an officer anymore."

"I'm sorry to hear that. I was really hoping you'd recover sufficiently to go back to work for the department."

"It wasn't to be. But I'm okay and working with disabled vets in Bethesda."

"I bet the work's a lot more rewarding than street cleaning in the capital."

"It is." Leigha realized for the first time that it really was. Her colleagues weren't badgering her about being the smallest cop on the force, and the patients were, for the most part, grateful for her assistance, not trying to shoot at her. For a woman who, at one time, could only see herself as a cop, she'd not only reimagined her life, she was living it and that made her feel pretty damn good. And the fact someone had tried to take away her newfound confidence by ramming into the back of her Jeep pissed her off. "I have a favor to ask."

"Anything," Caitlynn responded.

"Is it possible to find out if any of the criminals I've arrested, who were subsequently sentenced to prison, have come up for parole?"

"We have a database that collects that information. I'll have my secretary run a query."

"I'd appreciate anything you can give me." If the attack the night before was deliberate, she'd find the bastard.

"Why do you ask?"

"I'm curious."

"Casual curiosity, or something happened to you that makes you think you might be targeted for retribution?"

Leigha had always been impressed with Caitlynn's ability to see through the bullshit and get down to the nitty-gritty. "I was rear-ended last night."

"Fender bender?"

"Three times by the same vehicle."

"I see." Caitlynn paused. "I'll have my secretary get right on the task. In the meantime, you might want to stay with a friend or family."

Reaper had suggested the same, even volunteering to stay with her. Having the SEAL spend the night in her apartment would have been a complete disaster. "Thanks, Caitlynn. Anything you have will help."

"Be vigilant." The P.A. rang off, and Leigha stared at her cell phone for a long moment. Two people had given her the advice of staying with someone else. Maybe she was being too casual about the incident.

Her lunch hour over, she went back to work and kept busy for the rest of the day, working with warriors who had a lot more to deal with than she did. She focused on them and resigned everything else to the back of her mind for after she left work at the end of the day. Reaper's replacement showed up for his appointment slot, and Leigha couldn't help the twinge of disappointment, but she moved on, giving her new patient all the care and attention he deserved.

Perhaps Reaper would request a different therapist and save her the trouble of doing it herself. That would be just fine. She didn't need to be involved with him. He was far too dangerous to her mind and body.

REAPER SAT across the table from Hank Patterson at a bistro not far from the rehab facility.

Hank stared at Reaper's stump, shaking his head. "It's a shame you lost an arm, but I'm glad you're alive." He glanced up and smiled across the table.

Reaper fought the urge to wince, wondering how much time had to pass before he didn't feel a stab of pain over the loss of his arm. "Have you found anything yet?"

"My computer guy is still working on the search. Hopefully he'll have something by the end of the day."

"I appreciate the effort. Let me know what I owe you."

Hank waved a hand. "You don't owe me anything."

His hand fisted. "I don't need your charity."

"It's not charity. Consider it a brother helping a brother."

"I don't need help."

"Well, maybe I do."

Reaper snorted and stared across the table at Hank. "How can *I* help *you*?"

"Good to see you're staying in good shape." Hank nodded toward Reaper's left arm. "How's your aim?"

"Are you kidding me?" He waved his stump. "Gone."

Hank didn't rise to Reaper's angry response,

continuing with a calm tone, "What about your left hand?"

Surprised by his question and a little curious for the reason, Reaper shrugged. "Not as good."

"With practice, do you think you could fire expert?"

The image of the paper target passed through his mind. He shrugged. "Maybe."

Hank's jaw tightened and he leaned toward Reaper. "I need a *yes* or *no* answer."

"Yes," Reaper answered, suddenly sure. The short practice on the range the night before assured him he could do it in a relatively short amount of time. He just hadn't been ready to admit the fact, still somewhat unsure of his full capabilities. Like Leigha said, he had a lot more going for him than not.

Hank nodded and leaned back in his seat. "I have a proposition for you. A potential job offer."

Reaper raised his left hand. "If it's anything requiring me to sit behind a desk forty hours a week, thanks." He gave a definitive head shake. "But I'm not interested."

"I don't need a secretary. Already got one. What I need are trained SEALs who've experienced combat and aren't afraid of being shot at."

What in hell is he talking about? "For what purpose?"

"To provide security services to the clients of the Brotherhood Protectors."

Again, Reaper raised his hand. "I know what it stands for. But what would I do for the brotherhood? Mow the lawn, clean the gutters. I can't see where I'd be dodging bullets while trimming the shrubs."

Hank laughed. "You wouldn't be doing lawn maintenance. I need men like you as my agents."

Anger flared inside Reaper. Hank had to be playing a really cruel joke. "Are you forgetting something?" He waved his stump. "Nobody wants to hire a one-armed bodyguard."

"Let me handle the assignments. You concentrate on functioning as adeptly with one arm as most men can with two, and I'll put you to work." Hank stood. "I don't have time to stay and chat. I'll give you a ride back and then I have to head back to Montana. You don't have to give me an answer now. All I ask is that you think about it."

Reaper climbed into Hank's vehicle and rode back to his quarters in silence. He barely remembered what he said as he got out of the vehicle. For a long time, he stood on the curb and stared into the distance.

Bodyguard? Could he do everything a two-armed man was capable of? He thought back to the night before and how he'd fumbled to load rounds into the magazine. Yeah, the movements had been awkward, but he'd done the tasks on his own.

Leigha hadn't offered to help, and she hadn't stood by to laugh at his attempts. She'd left him in his booth to sink or swim.

And he swam. Awkwardly at first, but with increasing confidence as he learned how to work with his left hand.

Hope blossomed inside, and he quickly tamped it down, afraid to get too excited until he could prove to himself, he could do it. The only way he would, was to try. He hurried into the building, hoping to catch Leigha before she left for the day.

The rehab center was deserted, the benches clean, and the dirty towels picked up and put away. Disappointed he'd missed her, he stepped out in the hallway and ran into a petite blonde. He reached out to steady her.

"Reaper?" Leigha rested her hand on his chest and stared upward. "You really need to watch where you're going."

"Sorry."

"Did you need something?"

"I need you," he said, the scent of cotton candy wafting around him.

"You do?" she asked, her brows lowering. "Why?"

"I want you to take me back to the indoor range."

"Tonight?" She shook her head. "Can't you find someone else? I might not be the right person to hang out with."

"Has to be you. You're the only person who doesn't let me get away with crap."

She laughed. "That doesn't sound like a great recommendation."

"It's what I need." He took her hand in his. "Please. This is important."

Her eyes narrowed, and she bit her bottom lip. "As long as you promise me one thing."

Relief shot through him. "Anything."

She glanced around the hallway before lowering her voice and saying, "You can't kiss me."

"Done," he agreed. "I'll be strictly business."

Her gaze narrowed even more, her brows drawing together. Finally, she sighed. "Okay. Let me change into something besides scrubs. I'll meet you at my Jeep."

"Deal." He headed outside to wait. As he looked for her Jeep, he spotted a dark sedan drive out the other end of the parking lot. When the sedan's tires hit the main road, they squealed, and the vehicle raced away.

Someone was in a hurry to go home.

"I'm ready." Leigha appeared at his side,

dressed much as she was yesterday in jeans and a dark T-shirt with the DCPD logo printed over the left breast in gold. She'd removed the elastic band and let her hair flow around her shoulders in long golden blond tresses.

When she smiled up at him, the realization hit him like a punch to the gut. Damn, she was beautiful, and he was a fool to think he could remain unaffected. Still, he needed her assistance to get him into shape for Hank's job offer. "I have a huge favor to ask."

"As if going to the shooting range two nights in a row isn't big enough?"

"Sorry. You'll understand when I tell you what the favor is," he said.

"Come on, you can tell me as we walk." She took off across the pavement, her strides shorter than his but no less determined.

"I got a job offer."

She stopped walking and looked up at him, eyes wide. "That's fantastic. Who? What? Where? When do you start?"

Reaper laughed, feeling hopeful and yet more afraid of failing than he had been going through BUD/s brutal training. "A buddy of mine has a security firm. He said if I can do anything with one hand as well or better than a man with two, I've got the job."

Her brow wrinkled. "Security. Like a bodyguard?"

With a nod, Reaper took off toward her Jeep. "Yeah. If I can drive, shoot, and provide protection as well or better than other members of his team, he wants me to go to work for his company."

"What kind of men does he have on his team?"

"They're all former Navy SEALs."

Leigha whistled. "Wow."

His stomach clenched. "I think I can do this, if I can learn to use my left hand as well as I used my right."

"Starting with the shooting," she finished. "Other than taking you to the range, what did you want me to do?"

He cast a glance over his shoulder. "I want you to be my personal trainer."

"Wouldn't you be better off with another SEAL? Does your buddy have agents nearby you could pair up with to work out?"

His jaw tightened as he neared her Jeep and came to a stop. "I'm not ready to run with the pack."

"Okay." She nodded. "What kind of training do you want?"

"Full body. Running, squats, weights. Exercises to get me in shape and to get my left arm and hand ready to handle anything."

"Again, why me?"

He reached for her hand and held it in his palm, staring down at delicate, yet capable, little fingers. "You're the one who showed me I could do things on my own. You didn't coddle me, and you won't let me get away with wallowing in self-pity."

"A good personal trainer would do the same."

"Yeah, but he wouldn't look as good as you do in jeans and a T-shirt." Reaper winked. "I trust you."

She chewed on her bottom lip. "We'd have to work out after I get off duty at the rehab center."

"Every day."

"You'll also need practice driving, if you want to go into bodyguard work."

"Exactly. I can have my truck brought up from Little Creek as soon as I get clearance to drive from the doc."

"I don't know. This arrangement borders on crossing that line between therapist and patient. I could lose my job."

He held up his hand, palm out. "I promise not to kiss you."

She crossed her arms over her chest. "Damn right you won't."

"So, will you do it?"

She sighed and muttered, "I should have my head examined."

"Will you?"

"Yes."

He swept her into his arm and hugged her tight. "Thank you."

Leigha smiled, her face flushed and pink. "You promised."

"I didn't kiss you." He grinned. "You didn't say anything about hugging."

"You're a tricky bastard," she said, ducking her head to dig in her purse for her Jeep keys. Once she found them, she moved her thumb to activate the remote locks.

Before the button was pressed, something inside Reaper clicked. He grabbed the key fob, wrapped his arm around her waist, and ran backward with her clutched to his chest. When he was twenty yards away, he set her on her feet.

"What was that all about?" she asked.

"Maybe nothing." He held out his hand. "Let me have your keys."

She laid the keys in his palm.

He could be crazy but his gut told him better to be cautious than dead. Had he been more cautious in the village in Afghanistan, he might still be part of the SEAL team and digging sand out of his cracks in the Middle East.

The parking lot was nearly empty with only a

few vehicles scattered across an acre of spaces and nothing within a hundred feet of Leigha's Jeep.

"Back up and get down," he said.

"Why?" she asked.

"Just do it." His body tensed, his concentration focused on the Jeep.

Leigha took several steps behind him, stopped, and dropped to one knee.

"Lower." To demonstrate, he got down on his knees and dropped to his belly. "This low."

Reaper held up the key fob, sucked in a breath, and depressed the button to unlock the doors.

From the distance, he heard the door locks pop up. A pause of two seconds, and then the Jeep exploded in front of them, spewing debris as high as fifteen feet.

6

The concussion shook the ground. Reaper squeezed his eyes shut, dug his fingernails into the pavement, and waited for the ground to stop shaking.

The scent of desert dust filled his nostrils. The fog of debris surrounded him, and he could hear the shouting of his teammates. Tuck leaned over him. What was he shouting? Reaper couldn't hear him over the ringing in his ears. And the ground wouldn't stop shaking beneath him.

"Reaper!" a softer, gentler voice called out, piercing the persistent whining sound. Gentle hands pulled him over onto his back. "Reaper, you're okay, sweetie. You're okay. Open your eyes. You're in Maryland, not the desert. You're home. Open your eyes."

He drew on every last bit of his strength to open his eyes. The blue skies above contained no fog of dust. The face peering downward wasn't Tuck or Big Bird. It was Leigha, her brows puckered, her lips moving.

"You're okay," she said.

As the smoke and dust of his memories cleared, he realized the ground wasn't shaking but he was.

Leigha's hands smoothed over his left arm and cupped his face. "You saved my life."

Then everything came back in a rush. He sat up and pushed to his feet, ready to fight.

Sirens sounded, growing closer. People ran out of the hospital and rehab center. Soon, they were surrounded by a crowd.

A fire engine pulled into the parking lot, and firefighters dropped to the ground. Within ten minutes, they had the fire in what was left of Leigha's Jeep extinguished. Paramedics checked over Reaper and Leigha and didn't find anything more than minor scuffs and bruises.

Everyone congratulated them on averting a tragedy.

All the while, Reaper stood among the crowd, his head reeling, breathing rapidly, desperate to get away.

Leigha leaned close and whispered, "Come

with me." She took his hand and led him to the edge of the crowd.

A taxi pulled up in front of them and the driver leaned out the window. "You Ms. Fields?"

Leigha nodded. "I am." She opened the back door and motioned for Reaper to get in, and then she got in beside him. After giving the driver her address, she leaned against Reaper's arm, holding his hand in hers. Neither said a word. The entire journey to her apartment was conducted in silence.

By the time they got out and Leigha paid the driver, Reaper could breathe normally and the ringing in his ears had quieted. "Why did you bring me here?"

She hadn't let go of his hand the entire ride, and she wasn't letting go now. "After what happened, I don't think I can stay alone in my apartment. And I'd bet you wouldn't fare any better alone in your room." Leigha turned toward her building and walked away.

He didn't move, his hand pulling her to a stop. "You don't have to do this for me." God, he was mortified. She'd seen him lying on the ground, shaking like a frightened child. "I don't need your pity. I'm not afraid to be by myself."

"You might not be afraid, but I am." She turned back to face him. "What happened scared the shit out of me. I don't want to spend the night alone. Please..." Her blue eyes stared up into his. "Stay with me."

His chest tightened. How could he say no? "I can't stay." Reaper felt his resistance crumbling. He had to think of O'Connell. "I'm engaged."

"I know. I respect that. I'm not asking you to sleep with me. We can keep this purely platonic. I won't ask you to do anything you would be ashamed of tomorrow."

"Can't you call one of your brothers?"

"They have their own lives, three-and-a-half hours away. If whoever sabotaged my Jeep decides I'd be an easy target because I'm alone, my brothers couldn't get here in time." She stood for a long moment, staring into his eyes.

Reaper remained standing in the parking lot.

Leigha sighed. "You know, you're right. I'm asking too much of you." She gave him a weak smile and pulled out her phone. "I'll call the cab company and have the dispatcher send around another car. You should go back to your room and video chat your fiancée. I'll be fine. I sleep with my gun beneath my pillow. I'll be f—"

Something inside Reaper snapped. He closed the distance between them, tugged her hand, forcing her to fall against his chest. Then his hand dug into the hair at the back of her neck and he pulled, tipping back her head. "You don't understand. I can't stay with you because I'll want to do this." He claimed her mouth in a long, hard kiss, his lips moving over hers. His tongue lashed out, pushed past her teeth, and thrust against hers, twisting and tangling until he couldn't remember when he breathed last.

When at last he came up for air, he stared down into her glazed blue eyes and knew he was lost. "Now do you understand?"

Nodding, she took his hand, led him into her building, slipped the key into the lock, and opened her door.

He dragged her against him, and shoved her against the doorframe, bent, and scooped her up by the back of her thigh.

Leigha wrapped her legs around his middle and twined her arms around his neck. She kissed him, pulled on his lip with her teeth, and then thrust her tongue into his mouth.

God, she was hot, with her breasts smashed up against his chest, smelling of cotton candy and fresh air. With her, he didn't see or feel the heat of the desert, or smell the dust of a village so foreign to his home. That other hell, the one so hot it melted the soles of his boots, he only visited now in his nightmares.

LEIGHA KNEW what she was doing was wrong in so many ways. Yes, she'd been shot, yes, her life as a D.C. cop had been dangerous—facing thugs, gang members and sociopaths on a daily basis. But she'd never had someone try to blow her away with explosives. If Reaper hadn't asked her to help him...if he hadn't taken her keys at the last minute...

She shivered and delved deeper into the kiss. It wasn't enough. She needed to be closer, the kind of close that was skin-to-skin. Naked, bared to the touch, bared to the soul.

The explosion had shown her a vulnerable side to the big man. His anger she could take, the uncontrollable trembling brought on by the explosion had shaken her to the very core. PTSD was a frightening reality many soldiers lived with on a daily basis. His resistance to move past his disability and make it a capability had been her first hurdle with the man. She was afraid she couldn't help him with the deeper damage done in the explosion that had taken his arm and destroyed his trust in the world around him.

Right at that moment, held in his arms, with her back against the wall, she knew bringing him to her apartment was the only way she could solve both of their needs. He needed someone to be with him as badly as she needed to be with someone. Tomorrow, they'd face the consequences. Tonight, they would celebrate escape from what could have been a terrible tragedy. She brought up her head. "Close the door."

He lifted her with his single arm, stepped the rest of the way through the door, and kicked it closed behind him. Then he leaned her against the door, his mouth crashing down on hers.

Leigha welcomed him in, her tongue hungry for his, her body aching from the tips of her fingers to her core. By the swell of the ridge beneath his jeans, he was feeling it, too.

At the moment the kiss broke, she pushed against this chest. "Put me down."

He lowered her legs to the ground and bent to nibble her ear, trailing a line of kisses down the length of her neck to the base of her throat where her pulse beat wildly.

She reached for the waistband of his jeans. "Tell me no and I'll walk away," she whispered against his chest, inhaling the scent of his sexy aftershave as she prayed he didn't take her up on her offer.

He answered by twisting his fingers in the hem of her DCPD T-shirt and dragging it up her torso, her breasts, and over her head. He tossed it to the corner, reached behind her back, and fumbled with the clasp on her bra.

She didn't help him, knowing this task was as important to him as loading rounds into his weapon. Perhaps he felt that if he couldn't undress a woman, he wasn't a man.

Eventually, he pulled the hooks free and slipped the straps off her arms.

She let it fall to the floor, her breasts unbound for him to see, touch and taste.

Leigha's nipples tightened into hard little buds, as Reaper dipped his head and sucked one into his mouth. He flicked the tip with his tongue and rolled it between his teeth.

She arched her back, urging him to take more, to suck it deeper into his mouth. For each time he pulled, her core tightened in response until she ached for him to take all of her body.

Impatient for more sensation, she guided his head to her other breast. While he lavished his attention on it, she ran her hands down his back and dragged his T-shirt over his muscles. He raised his head and arm, and she tugged the garment over his head, dropping it to the floor.

With his torso bare, she could see all the muscles she rarely saw in his sessions. Tattoos covered much of his shoulders—bold dark lines and swirls in fantastical patterns, broken only by shrapnel scars incurred in the explosion that nearly took his life.

Leigha traced the patterns with her fingers, memorizing the images, the scars, and the hard planes of his toned muscles. He was beautiful from so many angles, and she wanted to explore them all.

With sharp moves, she kicked off her shoes and reached for the button on his jeans. The sooner they were naked, the better she'd feel. Slipping her hand inside the denim waistband, she flipped the button open and dragged down the zipper, careful not to catch his cock in the metal teeth. He swelled outward the farther down she went until his shaft burst free of the denim confines, the velvety smoothness resting in her palm.

He was long, thick, and firm. Leigha slipped her fingers along his length, marveling at the texture and firmness, ready to move to her bedroom and the next step in this seduction.

As if reading her mind, he took her hand and led her deeper into her apartment, moving with purpose toward the bedroom door. Once inside, he backed her up to the bed and eased her onto the mattress. Bending over her, he nibbled on a breast and tongued it thoroughly, then moved down her torso to the waistband of her jeans. He pushed the button through the hole and eased down her zipper

He scooted her body farther up the bed and dragged her jeans down her legs, past her thighs, knees, and ankles. When he had her on the mattress in only her panties, he straightened and stared at her body from the tips of her breasts to the V of material covering her mons, to the ugly scar on her knee.

Although she knew her reaction was ridiculous, she wanted to hide her scar. But she lay still, letting him drink his fill.

He reached out and touched the scar, tracing it from her lower thigh across her knee to her shin. "Does it still hurt?"

She shrugged. "On rainy days." Leigha reached out and took his hand, guiding it to her sex. "What aches now has nothing to do with gunshot wounds or knee replacements." She slipped his hand into her panties and left him to figure it out on his own.

He did, slipping his fingers between her folds to flick the stretch of flesh packed tightly with nerves.

Gasping, Leigha arched her back, digging her heels into the mattress. She raised her hips. "Again," she said. "Please."

Again, he stroked her and tingles rippled through her body, spreading from her core outward, to the tips of her fingers and toes. Reaper dragged her panties down her legs and off, then dropped to his knees, scooted her bottom to the edge of the bed, and kissed along her inner thigh.

She moaned, her sex tingling in anticipation,

quivering with excitement, because she was eager to feel the flick of his tongue on her most sensitive place.

And he delivered. Sliding his hand across the tuft of hair, he slipped inside, wet his finger, dragged it up to her clit, and swirled until she squirmed. Then he leaned closer and flicked her with his tongue, once.

She dug her fingers into his hair and urged him to do it again. "Please," she begged, spreading her thighs, drawing her heels up his backside. "Please," she repeated, her voice ragged, her body on fire, the need so great she would die if he didn't take her soon.

His relentless tonguing sent her over the top. Leigha, used to calling the shots in bed, conceded victory to Reaper as he launched her to the heavens, giving her the most incredible release she'd ever experienced. She rode the pleasure for as long as she possibly could. When she peaked and started down the other side, she clutched his shoulders and dragged him up her body. Next, she scooted back on the bed and spread her legs, offering herself, praying he'd take her up on the offer.

He stood beside her bed, his eyelids drooped to half-mast, but his nostrils flared like a bull preparing for a charge. "Protection?"

"In the drawer, I think." Dear Lord, she

prayed her stash was still there from a time she'd almost brought one of her classmate's home from school, desperate for company and sex. At the last minute, Leigha had changed her mind, realizing sex for the sake of sex was pretty pathetic. But a girl could never be too prepared.

He found a packet, tore it open, and worked the condom free.

Seeing him struggle, she reached for it.

But he held up his hand. "I have to be able to do everything myself, better than a man with two hands."

She laid back and smiled, her body humming with the afterglow of her orgasm. "So far, I'd give you an A+. But don't make me wait too long."

"On it." He slipped the condom over the head and down his incredibly long, thick shaft, in one fluid movement.

"Do you want me to be on top?" she offered.

"No. I have to do this right." He climbed up between her legs on his knees and leaned over her, balancing on one arm. He nudged her entrance with his cock, sliding the tip in and out, coating it in her juices.

His actions teased her until she wanted to scream. "Now," she whispered.

In one hard, swift thrust, he buried himself inside, driving deep all the way to his hilt.

He filled her channel, stretching her deliciously with his wide girth. For a long moment, he held himself inside, giving her body a chance to get used to him, to accommodate his size. Then he slid back out.

Leigha's channel contracted, dragging at him, willing him to come back inside. Another slow, steady glide in and out, and she was ready to scream. "Faster." She threw back her head, dug her heels into the mattress, and pushed up to meet him. "Sweet Jesus, faster."

He complied, hammering into her again and again, the thrusts so hard and furious that the headboard banged into the wall. He backed off only a little to keep from disturbing the neighbors, but continued his campaign to make her come a second time.

As her body tensed, his did, too. One last thrust sent her over the edge, flying into the land of tingling nerves and quivering body parts.

He buried himself so deep he became one with her body, his cock throbbing against her inner walls. His face was tense, his jaw tight as he spent his release. Then he lowered himself onto his elbow, his body lying on hers, but not with all of his weight crushing her.

"That was...incredible." Leigha sighed and snuggled closer.

"All I have to say is thank God for years of one-armed pushups."

A chuckle bubbled up her throat and escaped from her mouth. Then another.

His brow furrowed. "What's so funny?"

She stared up at him. "Nothing. I just feel... more alive than I've felt in a long time." She cupped his cheek in her hand. "And it feels pretty damned good." She tipped her head to the side. "Relax. You've already proved you can do better than any two-armed man."

With a huff of expelled breath, he rolled onto his right side.

She rolled with him, retaining their connection, enjoying the feel of him still thick and hard inside her body. When he relaxed beside her, she traced a scar close to his nipple. "Was that the first time you've had sex since the explosion?"

He nodded, his fingers caressing the swell of her breast.

Tingles ran over her skin. Leigha snuggled against him, her cheek resting against his chest. She yawned and closed her eyes. "Thank you for staying with me tonight."

"I couldn't let you stay alone." His voice grew distant.

Leigha knew what they'd done would have repercussions. He would have to deal with his conscience and his promise to marry another woman. She'd have to figure out how to manage his therapy without getting fired. But for tonight, she pushed all of those thoughts out of her mind and fell toward sleep, cradled in his arm. Tomorrow would come all too soon.

As she drifted, a cell phone rang in the other room.

Reaper slipped out of the bed and went to find it.

Leigha rolled into the spot where he'd been, enjoying the lingering warmth.

Then Reaper returned to the room, the phone in his hand, his magnificent body naked and ripped with muscles.

Leigha took a moment to see the pallor beneath the tanned skin of his face. "What's wrong?" she sat upright, pulling the sheet up over her breasts.

"O'Connell's been hit. They're bringing her back to the states tomorrow."

7

R eaper hovered beside O'Connell's bed, holding her hand in his. This was his close friend. He, Tuck, and O'Connell had been as tight as the Three Musketeers during training at Little Creek.

He barely recognized the woman covered in tubes and wires, her face pale against the hospital sheets. She didn't resemble the tough, confident spitfire Black Hawk pilot from the 160th Special Operations Aviation Regiment. She beat out five other male pilots to earn her spot on the Night Stalkers, ferrying navy SEALs and army Delta Force soldiers into harm's way. The only female to enter the boys club who'd scorned women from the get-go.

While O'Connell had been flying for her country, he'd been wallowing in his self-pity and cheating with his therapist. Last night, he'd laid next to Leigha, holding her petite body until morning, guilt squeezing his chest so tightly he couldn't breathe. He'd wanted to leave as soon as he'd gotten word about O'Connell. At the same time, he couldn't walk away from Leigha when someone was trying to kill her.

After he'd made love to her, he'd come to the conclusion he had to break off the engagement with O'Connell. Yes, he loved her. But he loved her like he loved Tuck. Their last kiss should have been a clue. There'd been no spark on his part. Nothing like when he kissed Leigha and his world lit up like the Fourth of July.

He feared he was falling for the feisty ex-cop, and now O'Connell was in serious condition. God, he couldn't break her heart, but he couldn't marry her knowing he didn't love her like she deserved to be loved. Fully, whole-heartedly, and definitely not like a buddy.

"Hey." O'Connell's eyes blinked open and she stared up at him. "What are you doing in Afghanistan? They letting one-armed SEALs back in?"

The sound of her voice loosened his worry a bit. He chuckled at her sass and leaned over to press a kiss to her forehead. "Welcome back to the States, sweetheart."

"Would rather have come on my own two

feet." She closed her eyes again, her breathing steady but shallow.

"It's a helluva way to get your pizza fix."

"Never go half-assed, I always say," she whispered. "I feel like I was hit by a truck."

"From what I heard, more like an RPG round."

"Think my insurance will cover the damage to my ride?"

"Yeah."

Her gaze traveled over his face. "How are *you*? You look better."

Just like O'Connell to ask how someone else was when she was laid up. "I've never been better."

She sighed. "I'm glad." Her eyes drifted closed again. "Cory?"

"Yeah, O'Connell?"

"When I'm able to stay awake..." her words faded.

Reaper thought she'd fallen asleep.

"...we need to talk," she finished on a sigh.

"We will. I promise." He touched her hand then waited until he was certain she was asleep before he left the room. Though they'd ridden to the center together in a rental car that morning, Reaper hadn't liked leaving Leigha even for the day. She'd be surrounded by people, but the explosion the night before meant her attacker knew where she worked and probably also knew where she lived.

Torn between being with O'Connell when she was so banged up and being with Leigha who was being terrorized, he headed for the rehab facility. Until he was certain Leigha was okay, he couldn't relax his guard.

When he entered the huge room of exercise equipment, therapists and veterans, he scanned the area, taking a minute to find her. She was smiling and laughing with the soldier she was helping work the range of motion of his right arm. She had him pretending to wash the windows of a tall building.

"Your wife will love you when she learns you can clean windows."

"Shh. Don't tell her. Let that be our little secret." He winked and went back to work pretend-cleaning the wall of imaginary windows.

Leigha turned, her eyes widening when she spotted him. Just as quickly, they narrowed. "It's not time for your session. What are you doing here?"

"I want you to reschedule my session for the end of day."

She shook her head. "Can't. We're short-handed, and the schedule is packed."

"Then don't go home without me."

Leigha glanced around and then back at

him. "We can't do this. I can manage on my own. You have to stay with your fiancée. I have my gun—"

"Where?'

"In my purse in the trunk of the rental car." Her mouth tightened into a grim line. "You know I can't bring it in here."

"It won't do you any good if whoever is attacking you gets to you before you get the gun out of the trunk."

"I'll have a security guard walk me to my vehicle."

"Just wait for me."

"No." She turned back to the man washing windows on the wall. "James, I'll be right back."

"I'm not going anywhere," he responded

Leigha led Reaper out of the big room and into a long sterile hallway. She didn't stop until they came to a door marked Cleaning Supplies. With a quick glance down the hallway, she pulled open the door, stepped inside, grabbed his hand, and yanked him in behind her. Once the door closed, she turned to face him. "What happened last night was incredible, amazing, and the best sex I've ever had."

Glad to hear that. He started to agree, but she held up her hand.

"But, it doesn't excuse the fact that I'm your therapist, you're my patient, and you're engaged to another woman. There can be no repeat performances."

"You can't stay alone."

"I've got that covered. My brother is coming in from D.C. to stay the weekend. I had a conversation with the police." Her fists bunched. "They're aware that last night was the second attempt on my life. They promised to have a unit cruise through my complex every hour each night until they catch the man responsible."

"What about here?"

"Like I said, I'll have security walk me out. I'll hit the unlock button far enough away, if a bomb is wired to the vehicle, I won't take the hit."

Reaper knew she was right and her precautions were spot on. "Have you heard anything from your contact about parolees?"

"Not yet, but I'll make that call again on my lunch hour." She sighed. "It has to be this way. We both have too much to lose."

He stared into her eyes, an ache building in his chest that threatened to steal his breath away. Even in her scrubs with her pale blond hair pulled back in a ponytail, no makeup on her face, she was beautiful. Reaper could still see her naked body beneath him, rising to take him deeper. He raised his hand to her cheek and brushed his thumb across the lips he'd kissed so thoroughly the night before. "If only things were different," he said.

Blinking fast, she cupped the back of his hand and leaned her cheek into his palm. "But they're not."

Reaper hated the way things were turning out. Just when he was getting his life back on track and daring to dream of a future. He bent to brush his lips across hers. "I'll miss this."

A moan slipped from her mouth, and she lifted her hand to cup the back of his neck. "I'll miss this." She rose onto her tiptoes and kissed him hard, her mouth slanting over his, her tongue darting out, pushing past his teeth to caress him in a long, sensuous glide.

When she broke away, she ducked past him, opened the door, and dashed from the cleaning supply closet.

Reaper waited a minute to give her time to get back to the rehab room, and then he left the closet. His cell phone vibrated in his pocket. He didn't want to answer it. Once again, his world seemed determine to crumble around him and he felt helpless to stop it. The phone vibrated again. What if the doctors were trying to get in touch to tell him O'Connell was in trouble?"

He jerked his phone from his pocket and noted the name on the screen. Hank Patterson. Reaper hit the Talk button, praying the man had news that could help him discover the source of Leigha's attacks.

"Reaper," Hank started without preamble. "Got some information for you on Fields's prior convictions."

"Shoot."

"Three have been paroled. One over six months ago by the name of Kimathi Jones. He's moved home to live with his family in North Carolina. Checks in regularly with his parole officer."

Check him off the list. "Who else?"

"Tyrone Bryant. Released last month. He lives with his mother in D.C. He's hit and miss reporting into his parole officer, but he did check in yesterday in person. In D.C."

Two down. "And the last guy?"

"He's the one I'm worried about. Jamal Clayton. Delivered to the halfway house in D.C. three days ago. They haven't seen him since."

His body stilled. "Did you obtain photos of him?"

"Sending now."

Reaper's phone buzzed, indicating an incoming text message. "Thanks. I'll pass this on to the local police."

"I heard about an explosion at the hospital in Bethesda," Hank said. "I hope your ex-cop friend wasn't involved."

"A near miss. She's okay, but he's getting way too close for comfort."

"Stay with her."

"You bet." Reaper leaned sideways, hoping to catch a glimpse of Leigha in the rehab room.

"Have you thought about my offer?"

"I have."

"And?"

"I'm working on it." He had to fight back a smile. "I'll let you know soon."

"We can use more men like you, Reaper."

He rang off and called the Bethesda Police Department. When he got the detective in charge of Leigha's case, he passed on the information he'd received from Hank.

"Thanks," the detective said. "You just saved us some time. We'll put out a BOLO on Clayton as a person of interest."

Reaper ended the call and slipped his phone into his pocket, feeling a little better, knowing the police force would be watching for Jamal. But, until he was captured and nailed for the attempts, Leigha wasn't safe.

No matter what her protestations were, Leigha couldn't go anywhere without some form of protection. Having her brother stay the night didn't get her from her work to her car, or from her car into her home. She was a tough little ex-cop, but someone had to have her six.

"Reaper!" A booming voice called out, jerking Reaper's attention from the tiles on the hospital floor to a group of men headed his way. "We didn't have to go far to locate you. The pretty blond in rehab said we might find you around here."

"Big Bird?' He squinted at the men headed his way. "Gator, guys..." Hell, the whole gang filled the corridor. Irish, Fish, Dustman, Nacho... It was like going through roll call. "What the hell are you doing here? I thought you guys were still in the sandbox."

Gator reached him first and hugged him, pounding him on the back. "Shipped back yesterday. We came to bring you your ride and check on Razor." He dropped car keys into Reaper's hand and stepped away to let the others in for a hug.

Big Bird nodded toward what was left of Reaper's right arm. "Hey, man. We're sorry about that."

Reaper shrugged. "I'm getting used to it. Besides, what have *you* got to be sorry about? You got me out alive. I couldn't ask for more."

Dustman snorted. "Tuck got you out. He refused to let any of us help."

With a frown, Reaper looked past his friends. "Speak of the devil, where is Tuck?" He missed his running buddy and roommate.

Big Bird shook his head. "He didn't come back with us."

"Didn't come to visit?" Reaper frowned. "What the fuck? Is he pissed about something?"

"You could say that," Nacho said.

Irish's usually cheerful face was grim. "We got bad intel again. Our informant set us up—the same source as what got you where you are."

"This time, they scored big," Big Bird added. "They shot down O'Connell's helicopter."

Dustman nodded. "I've never seen Tuck like he was."

"Yeah." Nacho got in his hug. "He stayed with O'Connell from the moment he found her until they loaded her into the C-130 for Landstuhl."

"Then he met with the Skipper and disappeared. I think he's on some super-secret mission," Big Bird said. "We think he's going after the dude who set us up."

Nacho shook his head. "He was *muy caliente* with the fire in his eyes."

Blood pounded in his ears, and Reaper's fist clenched. "Did he take any backup?"

Big Bird shook his head. "No."

"He's going after them alone?" Reaper closed his eyes and tilted back his head. "That dumbass. He needs someone to cover his six. No one should go it alone."

"You know we'd have gone with him, had we

known what he was up to." Big Bird's jaw was tight, his muscles bunched. "But we got orders to head home. And here we are."

Reaper should have been there. He and Tuck were tight. Surely, if he'd been by Tuck's side, he could have talked him out of going, or gone with him.

What could he tell O'Connell? She loved him as much as Reaper.

"So, where is O'Connell?" Nacho asked, looking around the hallway. "We want to make sure she pulled through."

"She's doing okay. I'll take you there. She might be happy to see your ugly mugs." He led the motley crew to the ward where O'Connell was just waking up.

She smiled and greeted them, one by one, until they all had a chance to touch her hand and wish her well. Then she glanced past them, her brow wrinkling, her gaze lingering on the doorway. When no one appeared, she turned to Reaper, her widened eyes filling with tears.

He shook his head. "Tuck's not coming."

A single tear slipped from the corner of her eye, down her cheek, and dropped to the pillowcase. "He made it out?"

Big Bird nodded. "He stayed at your side until you were shipped out of theater."

"Why didn't he come with you?" she asked.

"He stayed behind," Nacho said. "In Afghanistan."

Another tear followed the first, and she nodded.

"We need to let her rest." Reaper herded the men to the door and out into the hallway. "I'll be back," he promised her from the doorway, appalled to see the two tears were multiplying at an alarming rate.

"She didn't look so good," Big Bird said. "You sure she's going to be all right?"

Reaper nodded. "The doc says she'll be flying again soon."

Big Bird sighed. "Good to know. What about you?"

"I'm no good at flying helicopters," Reaper said with a smile, purposely answering the wrong question.

"You know what I mean. What's next for you?"

Reaper drew in a breath and forced a smile. "I'm embracing the civilian in me."

Dustman snorted "What the fuck does that mean?"

He grinned. "I'm looking at an opportunity. I hope to start a new job in the next month or so. I just have to get through some more therapy and learn to live one-armed."

"Is it hard?" Nacho asked then glanced away.

"We had tougher training in BUD/s." Reaper clapped Nacho on the back. "I can do anything I set my mind to." One strong-willed therapist had taught him that. He glanced at his watch. She wouldn't be off for another couple of hours. "How long are you guys staying?"

"We have to leave soon." Big Bird glanced at his watch and his lips tightened. "We're still on call, despite just getting back, and the skipper expects us in Little Creek by nightfall."

"Thanks for bringing my truck. I'm glad you came to see us. It means a lot to me, and I know O'Connell was glad, too."

"Take care of her." Dustman nodded toward O'Connell's closed door. "She's hauled our rangy asses out of more than one hot situation."

"I know. I'll keep an eye on her," Reaper promised.

The team left Reaper standing in the hall, watching as they walked toward the bank of elevators. They looked strange in the clean, white, sterile hallway, their broad shoulders stretching across the corridor. His heart hurt all over again. One damned explosion had taken away so much. His arm, his career and, most of all, his family. God, he'd miss deploying with them. He'd miss the pranks they played on each other and the camaraderie.

Reaper pushed through the door into O'Connell's room. He couldn't focus on what he'd lost. He'd miss them, but he'd get on with his life, even if doing so killed him. Leigha had gone through a similar situation and come out with a new purpose to her existence. She was helping others. If she could do it, he could, too.

"Cory?" O'Connell hit the button to raise her head a little.

He hurried forward and pulled a chair up to the side of her bed. "Feeling any better?"

She nodded. "A little. We need to talk."

"We can wait until you're up and running circles around me. I've got all the time in the world." As long as he could leave with Leigha tonight when she got off duty. He took her hand in his. "Ladies first."

She stared at his face, the tracks of tears still evident on her cheeks, her eyes red-rimmed. "Remember when you asked me if I felt anything when we kissed?"

He nodded, his belly clenching. He'd been about to tell her he couldn't marry her.

"I lied." Her gaze slipped to where he held her hand. "I didn't feel anything."

He frowned. "Then why did you lie?"

Biting her lip, she looked away. "You were in a bad place...I didn't want to upset...Hell, Cory, I love you."

The noose around his chest contracted,

making it hard for him to breathe. How could he tell her he couldn't marry her when she had just professed her love?

O'Connell squeezed his hand and stared into his eyes. "I love you like a brother."

He sagged over her hand, the air filling his lungs in a whoosh. Relief danced through him.

"Cory?" She tugged his hand. "Say something. Please, please, don't hate me. I promised to marry you, and if that's what you really want, I'll go through with it. But I don't love you like you deserve to be loved."

He lifted his head, a chuckle rising up his throat that he couldn't contain. She didn't love him. A heavy weight lifted, and he looked up, his gaze meeting hers.

She glared. "What's so damned funny?"

"I was going to tell you the same thing." He lifted her hand to his lips and pressed a kiss to the back of her knuckles. "I love you, too, O'Connell. Like I love Tuck and Big Bird, Nacho, and Fish. You're one of the guys, a great friend, someone I can count on to stand by me. And you can count on me to stand by you."

She lay back, closed her eyes, and smiled. "Thank God."

"So, you never loved me?" he asked, thinking back over the past months.

Her eyes opened again, and she shook her head. "Not like you wanted me to love you."

"I thought I loved you, but I think I was more in love with the idea of getting married and having someone to come home to."

O'Connell snorted. "Like that would ever happen. I'll never be a typical housewife. I'm lucky to call any place home for more than a few months at a time. Anyone who got involved with me would have to take a backseat to my job."

"Same goes for a SEAL." He shook his head. "All the time we were engaged and neither of us knew how to break it off."

"So, what made your realize I wasn't the one for you?" She raised her brows and then squinted. "Have you found the right one?"

His first thought was of Leigha, her petite, naked body stretched across the bed, her legs parted, her blue eyes smoky, beckoning him.

"You don't have to answer." She smiled. "I can see it in your eyes and the way you smile when you're thinking about her. Who is she? I have to meet the special woman who captured my fiancée's heart while I was away."

He shrugged, suddenly glad for someone to talk to about Leigha. "I'm not in love with her. We haven't even been out on a first date. But I feel different when I'm around her."

"How different?"

"More determined. She makes me want to be a better person."

"You're pretty awesome already."

"What about you? How did you know I wasn't the guy for you?"

Again, she looked away and tugged on the hem of the sheet.

Then the truth hit him. Tuck had practically bit his head off the day before the mission that ended Reaper's career. He'd told Reaper O'Connell wasn't the right woman for him. "You're in love with Tuck?"

She didn't look at him, but the real tears welling in her eyes and spilling down her cheeks was confirmation enough.

"Oh, babe. Have you told him?"

"No." She reached for a tissue but couldn't quite grab it.

Reaper lifted the box and laid it on the bed beside her. "Why not?"

"I was too busy saying *yes* to another man's proposal." She sniffed and a fresh wave of tears spilled from her eyes. "Now he's gone on some stupid mission without any of his teammates to cover for him." With a shaky hand, she pressed the tissue to her eyes. "What if he doesn't come back?"

"Are you kidding? Tuck's a cat. He's got nine lives. I don't think he's gone through but maybe two, tops. He'll be back." Reaper prayed he was right. He hated being the reason his two best friends hadn't gotten together yet. "Hey, the doc's gonna skin me alive if he finds you crying. You should be recovering, not blubbering like a baby."

She glared through her tears. "I'm not blubbering."

He handed her another tissue. "Then wipe the snot from your nose and get well soon. You have to look better than you do right now if you want Tuck to notice you. He's got an eye for *pretty* blondes."

She gave a half-hearted, weak attempt at throwing the tissue his way. "Whoever your new girl is, she's lucky to have you, despite your lousy attempts to cheer me up."

"I know." He winked and rose. "What you need is some sleep. Let your body recuperate. I have something I need to do. I'll see you in the morning."

"Cory?"

He stopped at the end of her hospital bed. "Yeah, babe."

She gave him a crooked smile. "Thanks for understanding."

Reaper smiled. "We're just two messed-up people, aren't we?"

"Yes, we are." She laughed.

His heart lighter, Reaper headed back to his room to shower and change into clean jeans and a T-shirt. He planned on taking Leigha home that night in his truck. Whoever had planted the explosives the night before in her Jeep wouldn't know to do the same to his truck. He'd get her safely to her place and hopefully send her brother home. He had Leigha's six and would make sure whoever had it out for her didn't touch her.

8

—————

The patients were gone and most of the therapists had departed for the day, leaving Eric and Leigha to do the last walkthrough before turning out the lights.

Though she'd told him she would call a security guard to walk her to her rental car, Leigha had been watching the door for the past thirty minutes, waiting for Reaper to appear. So far, he hadn't. Didn't he know the center closed thirty minutes early on Friday? The extra time gave the staff and patients a fighting chance to get home before the big evening traffic jams hit.

Oh, well, Eric was still there, he could walk her to her car. Not that she needed him. As an ex-cop, she could take care of herself. Or so she kept telling herself. Yesterday had been a real eye-opener. If Reaper hadn't been there, they'd have been piecing her together, if she didn't die from the explosion. A shiver rippled across the back of her neck.

"Ready?" Eric asked with his hand poised on the light switch.

"I am." Leigha stepped out in the hallway where a janitor had gotten a jump on the nightly cleaning and was running the floor polisher, the sound echoing off the walls, making conversation difficult. "Did you turn off the light in your office?"

Eric frowned, his hand on the doorknob, ready to pull it closed. "I think I did. Hell, I'll be right back. I can't remember if I did or didn't."

Leigha slid her purse up her shoulder and smiled. "No hurry."

"Don't go anywhere. I'm walking you to your car." He shook his head. "I still can't believe someone stood out in the parking lot and wired your car with explosives, but no one saw him. I'm just glad you weren't injured. It blows my mind." He pointed at her. "Stay."

"I'm not going anywhere," she assured him.

The janitor in his coveralls worked his way backward toward her, sweeping the machine back and forth across the wide hallway.

Leigha glanced toward the other end of the corridor, still hoping to see Reaper headed her way. She moved closer to the wall as the janitor came abreast of her position. The machine shut off, and Leigha turned to greet him with a smile.

Her heart slipped to her knees when she looked into his dark eyes and recognized a face from her past.

Jamal Clayton sneered and pointed a pistol at her belly. "I've waited a long time for this."

Leigha took a step backward, running into the wall behind her. "How did you get in here?"

"Walked right in, carrying a box of cleaning supplies I stole from the back of a van." Clayton laughed. "No one stopped me. No one checked to see what was in the box." He waved the pistol toward the exit. "Let's go."

She shook her head. "I'm not going anywhere with you."

"Have it your way. I sure hate to make a mess of the floors I just waxed." He shrugged and aimed the gun at her chest. "I was going to give you a chance to run, a chance you didn't give my brother."

Her chin jutted upward. "Your brother was about to kill me after he'd already shot me in the knee. He wasn't running, because he was coming back to finish me off."

A shoulder lifted then dropped. "That's not how I saw it."

"Well then, you saw wrong."

His lip curled back. "Shut up, bitch. He was my brother. You broke my mother's heart."

"You and your brother did that to your mother by your actions."

"Leigha, you were right. I hadn't turned out—"

"Get back, Eric!" Leigha shouted and swung her purse at Clayton. But she missed.

Clayton turned and fired.

Eric's eyes widened and he clutched his middle, and then he dropped to the floor.

Anger ricocheted with adrenaline through Leigha, and she kicked with her new knee, her heel hitting Clayton's wrist. The gun flew from his hand, landed on the slick tile floor, and slid toward the wall.

Leigha dove for it, landing hard on her stomach, and skidded toward it. She almost had it when Clayton grabbed her ankle and jerked hard, pulling her away from the gun.

She rolled to her back and would have kicked him, but he landed on top of her before she could cock her leg.

Clayton straddled her hips and grabbed her throat, squeezing tight.

Her air cut off, Leigha swung her fists, catching him in the chin, the neck, anywhere she could, but her arms were shorter than his, and her blows weren't enough to convince him to let her go. She bucked and thrashed, but the lack of oxygen made her vision blur and the lights above fade. Damn it, she couldn't let him win! She had to get help for Eric. She wanted more time with Reaper.

This couldn't be the end.

Clayton jerked to the side, rolling her with him, his hands loosening enough for Leigha to thrust hers up between his arms and knocked them away.

That's when she saw why Clayton had been thrown to the side.

Reaper towered over the bastard, his face a mottled vision of rage.

Clayton swept his feet to the side, aiming for Reaper's ankles, in an attempt to knock him off his feet.

Reaper stepped back in time and landed a kick to the man's side. "It's over, Jamal. You've just earned a one-way ticket back to jail."

"Fuck you." He rolled to his knees and launched himself toward the gun.

Leigha beat him to it, snatched it from the ground, and aimed it at his chest. "You're done." Her actions were steady and sure.

"I'm going to kill you," he said through his teeth. "Like you killed my brother."

"Not today, you're not," she said, holding the weapon steady.

Clayton started to his feet, his muscles bunching.

Reaper grabbed the man's arm, yanked it up behind his back, and shoved him face-first against the wall.

The man hit hard, nose-first, blood gushing out, spraying across the white tile floor.

Reaper leaned his weight against the man, holding up his arm between his shoulder blades. "You're not killing anyone. Not tonight."

"Can you hold him?" Leigha asked, her gun still pointed at her attacker as she moved toward Eric, lying on the floor in the open door of the rehab unit.

"Do what you have to," Reaper said. "He's not going anywhere."

Leigha pulled her cell phone out of her purse and dialed 911, reported the incident, and requested medical support stat. Then she knelt beside Eric.

"I don't think I'll be walking you to your car this evening," he said, holding his hand tight against the wound. Blood stained his fingers.

"Don't worry about me. I have another body-guard on standby." She shot a glance at Reaper. "Let me take over here."

"I think he's ready to graduate from rehab," Eric said.

Leigha applied pressure to the wound. "I'd

like to transfer him to another therapist when you get back to work."

"Why's that?"

"I've committed the ultimate sin."

Eric nodded and gave a weak grin. "Fell for him, didn't you?"

"I didn't plan on it."

He chuckled. "It happens."

The police arrived and took Clayton in custody, reading him his rights as they led him away.

Two paramedics entered behind the police and took charge of Eric's care. They applied a pressure bandage to the wound, slipped an oxygen mask over his face, and established an IV. When they had him stabilized, they moved him to the waiting ambulance.

Reaper insisted on the medics checking her over. She did let them, just to make him shut up. Secretly, she was glad he cared enough to make sure she was all right. Then he slipped his arm around Leigha's waist and held her against him while the police questioned them both. When everyone cleared out, he walked her to his truck and opened the door.

"I should take my rental car." She pointed toward the parking lot.

"No," Reaper said. "Get in."

She frowned. "Bossy, are we?"

He smiled, holding the door "Please. Will you let me take you home?"

Leigha hesitated. If he took her home, there was only one thing that could happen once they got there. "Clayton's not a problem now that they have him in custody. I don't need a bodyguard."

"I didn't ask if you wanted a bodyguard. I asked if you'd let me take you home." His lips twitched. "It's a *yes* or *no* answer."

With *no* on the tip of her tongue, she opened her mouth and said, "Okay."

"Okay, you'll let me take you home, or okay you want a bodyguard?" He chuckled. "Don't answer, just get in."

"By the way...nice truck." She climbed into the cab and buckled her seatbelt.

Reaper climbed into the driver's seat, reached across with his left hand to shift into reverse, and backed out of the parking space. He stopped and shifted into drive, reaching across the steering column to manage the gears.

"You can have your steering column fitted with left-hand shift," she said. This would be the first time she'd been in a vehicle with him and he was doing the driving.

"I like it the way it is."

"Suit yourself." She leaned back against the plush leather seat and let the stress of the past couple of hours seep from her body. "By the way, thank you for saving my life. Again."

He nodded without speaking.

"I asked Eric to reassign you to another therapist."

That got Reaper's attention. He straightened and shot her a narrow-eyed glance. "I don't want another therapist."

"For that matter, he suggested you were ready to graduate."

Reaper shook his head. "You promised to work with me until I could do anything a two-armed man could do as good or better. The doc assigned me another three weeks of therapy. You're not quitting on me now. I still need you."

And I'm falling in love with you, you big dufus. Leigha bit down hard on her tongue to keep from saying what was really on her mind. "How's your fiancée?" *Wow. Did that sound as catty to him as it did to me?*

"O'Connell is doing better, and she's not my fiancée."

And just like that, hope blossomed through her chest. Try as she might, she couldn't keep the feeling from spreading. "Was it something you said? I can completely imagine you sticking your foot in your mouth." She turned toward the window, but a reflection caught her attention. The dark lights from the dash made the window a mirror, reflecting her face as well as his. She leaned back and studied his face with a sideways glance.

"We weren't in love with each other."

That made her glance at him directly. "I don't understand. Then why were you engaged?"

"I only *thought* I loved her. Turns out I don't."

"So, what was *her* story? Or did she realize she wasn't the girl for you when you told her you didn't love her?"

"Worse." Shaking his head, he smiled. "She felt sorry for me when I lost my arm. She's in love with my best friend, Tuck."

"Oh. That hurt." Leigha sat back, her tongue strangely tied, her heart racing, a hundred questions warring to be asked first, and all of them too direct, too revealing of her own emotions and desires. So, she sat like a lump, wanting to ask, but afraid of the answers. Never in her life had she been so filled with so much indecision and angst. The man was making her into a mess.

When they arrived at her apartment complex, she didn't wait for him to open the door. Instead, she slid out of her seat. "Thanks for the ride. I guess I'll see you Monday for your next session."

He dropped to the ground and met her at the front bumper. "Did you forget that you promised to give me therapy sessions after hours?"

"Uh, about that." Her stomach rolled, and she looked up at him. "I can't."

"Can't or won't?" He stepped up to her and took her hand, lacing his fingers with hers.

She moaned. "Do you have any idea what you're doing to me?"

"I hope I do." He winked and tugged her hand, bringing her body up against his. "Otherwise, I'm wasting my best moves." He bent his head.

But she raised a finger to his lips. "One more question."

He laughed. "Okay. But only one."

She drew in a deep breath and released it before asking, "How did you know you didn't love her?" Leigha dropped her hand to his chest, her heart thumping, her breath caught in her throat.

"Because of the kiss." He lowered his head and swept his lips across hers. "No sparks."

Her lips tingled, sending electrical impulses through her system like miniature shockwaves. Her core radiated heat and her sex throbbed.

He abandoned her mouth and kissed a path across her jaw and down the long line of her neck.

She let her head fall back, giving him better access to the pulse pounding at the base of her throat. "And did you find someone who makes you spark?" Sweet Jesus, she was on fire!

"Uh-huh." He raised his head, his mouth returning to hers, and he kissed her, long, hard, and so thoroughly she was breathless when he let her up for air. "She inspires a veritable array of fireworks."

"Anyone I know?"

"Maybe."

"That was a *yes* or *no* question."

"Then *yes*." He glanced at her building. "I promised to take you home."

"And you did."

"We're not there yet."

"Not nearly," she agreed.

"Then let me fulfill my promise." He took her hand and led her to her door.

Gaze locked on his, she opened it. Once again, they didn't make it inside without another mind-blowing kiss in the open doorway. Leigha wrapped her arms around his neck and said, "I'm not completely home until I'm over the threshold."

He scooped her up in his arm and carried her home.

9

R eaper stood in front of the mirror, adjusting his tie.

"Are you sure this is how you want to do this? You don't want to have it in a church surrounded by all your buddies from SEAL Team 10?" O'Connell stood behind him in a cream-colored dress, her hair pulled up in a fancy twist that women liked to wear. She looked more like a girl than a seasoned helicopter pilot.

"Humor me, will ya?" Reaper waved his stump of an arm, the surgical scars thick and ragged. "I'll have the people who mean the most to me here."

He was nervous, excited and wound up tighter than a top. This was the best day of his life and his friends had made sure he lived to experience it. Not only was today his last day at Bethesda, it was his wedding day.

The only thing that could make this day better was if his best friend arrived in time to stand in as his best man. He'd tried many times to contact Tuck via video chat, text, email and cell phone. Whatever mission he was on, he wasn't responding.

Reaper gave up and passed his message on to Tuck's commander, asking him to make sure Tuck got back to the States in time for his wedding. He asked him to tell Tuck that he had a tux with his name waiting. Be there.

Now Reaper stood in the rehab center, surrounded by the doctors, nurses, and other veterans who'd been with him throughout his recovery.

A loud click sounded, and Mendelssohn's *Wedding March* blared through the speaker system.

"Wait." Reaper waved with what was left of his right arm, his jacket sleeve pinned to keep it from flapping. "He's not here yet." How could he start his wedding without his best man?

"Who's not here?" O'Connell asked, her eyes narrowing.

"My best man. He promised he'd be here on time." Having Tuck stand at his side would make his day complete. And if he wasn't mistaken, the event would make O'Connell's as well. "His plane landed over an hour ago. He should be here by now."

The door to the therapy room crashed open, and a tall man dressed in the U.S. Navy service dress blue uniform burst through. "Am I too late?"

Eyes wide, O'Connell pressed a hand to her chest. "Tuck?"

Reaper grinned. His plan was coming together nicely. "Tuck! You made it!" He motioned Tuck forward with his stump. "About damned time. The ceremony's about to start. Get up here."

Tuck didn't move. His gaze fixed on O'Connell. "I wasn't going to come, but Skipper insisted."

"Not come to my wedding?" Reaper's grin broadened. He couldn't have planned this day better. Not only was he marrying the woman of his dreams, he was getting his two best friends together where they belonged. "You'd skip out on seeing your best bud shackled with an old ball and chain?"

Tuck glared, his lips pulled into a tight line. "She's not a ball and chain. Any man would be proud to have her as his wife."

O'Connell, her hand still pressed to her breast, bit her lip, silent tears trickling down her cheeks. "Cory, you didn't tell me he was coming."

"I know." Reaper winked, his chest puffing out. He leaned toward her and whispered, "I wanted to surprise you." To Tuck, he said, "Are you standing by me, or do I have to ask Schotzy to fill in?"

A large man in scrubs stepped forward. "I'd be happy to."

"Stand down. Let the man decide first." Reaper gave Tuck a chance to speak up. "What's it to be? You've been my best friend since BUD/s. I don't want to do this without you by my side, but I will."

"I came to stop this wedding." Shoulders held back, Tuck marched toward Reaper and O'Connell.

The people gathered in the room emitted a collective gasp.

Reaper summoned his best surprised look, fighting the grin pulling at the corners of his lips. "Why would you stop me from marrying the girl I love?"

Tuck's fists clenched and a muscle ticked in his jaw. "Because you can't marry her."

Reaper turned from Tuck to O'Connell. "Why? Is she already married, and I didn't know?"

"No." Tuck's jaw tightened.

Reaper bet he could chew nails about now, but he wasn't cutting his buddy any slack. If he wanted O'Connell, he had to tell her. "She agreed to marry me. I love her." He waved his left hand. "What more confirmation do I need?"

Tuck's cheeks flushed a ruddy red and his nostrils flared. "She doesn't love you."

"That's news to me." Leigha stepped through the waiting crowd, wearing a simple white wedding dress that hugged her petite figure perfectly. She wore her hair loose, hanging down her back like Reaper liked it. He couldn't wait to get her back to their place and run his hand through its length.

But he had a wedding to attend and a buddy to shake up. And damned if he wasn't doing a good job of it, based on the way Tuck's jaw slackened.

"Who's she?" Tuck asked, jerking his head.

"Uh, Tuck..." O'Connell's lips twitched, and a smile spread across her face. "You've been in dark ops too long. I take it you haven't talked to Cory in a while, and there's been a...uh...change of plan."

He glanced at her, his brows twisted. "I don't understand. I came to stop you from making the biggest mistake of my life."

"The biggest mistake of *your* life?" Reaper asked. "And what would that be?"

Taking a deep breath, Tuck faced Reaper. "Marrying Delaney."

O'Connell stood taller and slipped her arm through Reaper's. "I happen to think Cory would make a terrific husband." She nodded toward Leigha standing at the far side of the room, slowly walking toward them with the wedding march still playing. "A terrific husband for Leigha."

"Who's Leigha?" Tuck demanded, his gaze shifting between his friends.

Reaper had a really hard time holding back his laughter at his friend's expense.

"Shh." Leigha pressed a finger to her lips and picked up the pace, marching up to Tuck. "Please stop yelling. You're disturbing the patients."

Reaper's joy spread across his face. He had the woman he loved at his side. And he would marry her in front of the people he cared most about. "Are we disturbing anyone?"

Everyone in the room shouted. "No!"

"Marry her already!" Jason, a triple amputee in a wheelchair, shouted. "We want to see the kiss."

Frowning, Tuck faced O'Connell. "I don't understand."

She shook her head, still smiling. "Cory's marrying Leigha, his physical therapist."

"I came to stop him from marrying *you*."

Poor Tuck had that deer-in-the-headlights look. "You're a little late for that." Reaper finally relented. Tuck had suffered enough. "We broke our engagement shortly after O'Connell arrived at Bethesda. You'd know this fact if you hadn't gone off all dark ops on us." He shook his head. "O'Connell doesn't love me."

"Yes, I do." O'Connell chuckled and pecked Reaper's cheek. "Like a brother. And since he doesn't have any siblings or relatives, someone had to look out for his well-being."

O'Connell took a step toward Tuck, but before she could get to him, Leigha stuck out her hand. "I'm Leigha. You must be Tuck." She grinned. "You're just like Reaper described you."

Tuck glared at Reaper. "And when would you have told me you two called it off?"

Reaper shrugged. "I'd have told you sooner, if I'd known you cared." He glared back at Tuck, still mad at him, even though he was glad to see him, alive and well. "But you seemed hell-bent on volunteering for every suicide mission they could come up with. And you never returned any of my messages. I figured you had some bug up your ass about her."

"So, you fell in love with Leigha?" Tuck asked.

Reaper smiled. "I did." He held out his hand.

Leigha joined her hand with his and leaned against him. "I didn't like him at first. He was very grouchy. Then when we got the pain under control, he turned out to be such a flirt with all the ladies. I had a hard time trusting him."

"She fell for my charm and good looks." Reaper smiled down at her. "And the tattoo of Daisy Mae on my ass."

Leigha rolled her eyes. "No, I fell, and you helped me up with your injured arm, even though I knew it hurt like hell." She shook her head, a sweet smile playing across her lips.

Reaper nearly laughed at her story. Eric stood nearby, shaking his head. He'd been there as well as Reaper. Leigha had more than fallen. She'd been attacked and nearly killed.

God, he loved this ex-cop who played down her incredible bravery in the face of death.

Leigha went on with her bullshit, glossed-over tale, played out for the benefit of their friends and patients. "I figured if you could sacrifice a little pain to help me up, you couldn't be all bad. Maybe half bad. And that's just the way I like you. Half bad boy, half gentleman. One hundred percent SEAL." She stood on tiptoe and kissed him full on the lips. "Now, are you marrying me, or do I have to return this dress for a refund?"

Reaper grinned. There was the sass he loved so much. "Let's have a wedding!"

They skipped straight to the *I do's*. And the

best part: Reaper got to kiss the bride. He took his time, drank his fill, and went back for seconds. This was the woman who lit the whole damned box of fireworks in his books.

He nibbled on her ear and whispered, "Wanna go back to our place and get started on the wedding night?"

"Umm, that's a distinct possibility," she answered. "But what about our guests?"

Reaper glanced around the room. His SEAL Team 10 teammates were swapping war stories with patients, laughing and sharing experiences. For some of the patients, the happy occasion would help to take their minds off their own problems.

O'Connell and Tuck were holed up in the corner making up, which made Reaper's heart swell. Those two should have been together all along. "I don't think we'll be missed," Reaper pronounced. "Come on." He grabbed Leigha's hand and headed for the exit.

As he started through the door, he spotted Hank stepping through, a smile on his face. "I hear congratulations are in order." He hugged the bride and shook Reaper's hand.

"In more ways than one." Leigha smiled at the man. "Don't tell me you have his first assignment, and we're just starting our honeymoon."

Hank's smile faded. "No worries. Another

Brotherhood Protectors agent will cover for him until you get back."

"Will my client have an issue with my being one hand short of a pair?" Reaper quipped, too happy to be disappointed if the answer wasn't what he wanted to hear.

"Not at all. I think the client will just be happy to have someone to protect him." Hank waved toward the door. "Go on. Enjoy your honeymoon."

Before anyone else could waylay them, Reaper hustled Leigha out the door and into their new life together. He never would have guessed that by losing his arm, he'd gain the love of his life.

THE END

WYATT'S WAR

HEARTS & HEROES SERIES BOOK #1

New York Times & *USA Today*
Bestselling Author

ELLE JAMES

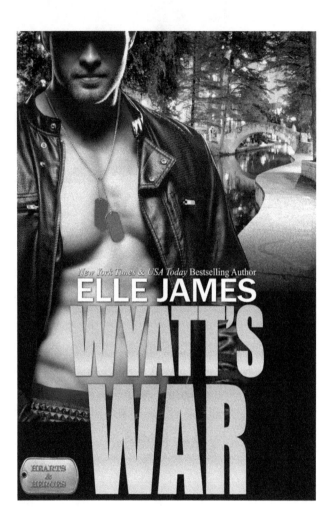

New York Times & USA Today Bestselling Author

ELLE JAMES

WYATT'S
WAR

HEARTS
&
HEROES

1

———

Sergeant Major Wyatt Magnus pushed past the pain in his knee, forcing himself to finish a three-mile run in the sticky heat of south Texas. Thankfully his ribs had healed and his broken fingers had mended enough he could pull the trigger again. He didn't anticipate needing to use the nine-millimeter Beretta tucked beneath his fluorescent vest. San Antonio wasn't what he'd call a hot zone. Not like Somalia, his last *real* assignment.

It wouldn't be long before his commander saw he was fit for combat duty, not playing the role of a babysitter for fat tourists, politicians and businessmen visiting the Alamo and stuffing themselves on Tex-Mex food while pretending to attend an International Trade Convention.

The scents of fajitas and salsa filled the air,

accompanied by the happy cadence of a mariachi band. Twinkle lights lit the trees along the downtown River Walk as he completed his run around the San Antonio Convention Center and started back to his hotel. Neither the food, nor the music lightened his spirits.

Since being medevaced out of Somalia to San Antonio Medical Center, the combined armed forces' medical facility, he'd been chomping at the bit to get back to where the action was. But for some damn reason, his commander and the psych evaluator thought he needed to cool his heels a little longer and get his head on straight before he went back into the more volatile situations.

So what? He'd been captured and tortured by Somali militants. If he hadn't been so trusting of the men he'd been sent to train in combat techniques, he might have picked up on the signs. Staff Sergeant Dane might not be dead and Wyatt wouldn't have spent three of the worst weeks of his life held captive. He'd been tortured: nine fingers, four ribs and one kneecap broken and had been beaten to within an inch of his life. All his training, his experience in the field, the culture briefings and in-country observations hadn't prepared him for complete betrayal by the very people he had been sent there to help.

He understood why the Somali armed forces

had turned him over to the residual al-Shabab militants that were attempting a comeback after being ousted from the capital, Mogadishu. He might have done the same if his family had been kidnapped and threatened with torture and beheading if he didn't hand over the foreigners.

No, he'd have found a better way to deal with the terrorists. A way that involved very painful deaths. His breathing grew shallower and the beginning of a panic attack snuck up on him like a freight train.

Focus. The psych doc had given him methods to cope with the onset of anxiety that made him feel like he was having a heart attack. He had to focus to get his mind out of Somalia and torture and back to San Antonio and the River Walk.

Ahead he spied the pert twitch of a female butt encased in hot pink running shorts and a neon green tank top. Her ass was as far from the dry terrain of Somalia as a guy could get. Wyatt focused on her and her tight buttocks, picking up the pace to catch up. She was a pretty young woman with an MP3 device strapped to her arm with wires leading to the earbuds in her ears. Her dark red hair pulled back in a loose ponytail bounced with every step. Running in *the zone*, she seemed to ignore everything around but the path in front of her.

Once he caught up, Wyatt slowed to her pace,

falling in behind. His heart rate slowed, returning to normal, his breathing regular and steady. Panic attack averted, he felt more normal, in control and aware of the time. As much as he liked following the pretty woman with the pink ass and the dark red, bobbing ponytail, he needed to get back and shower before he met the coordinator of the International Trade Convention.

Wyatt lengthened his stride and passed the woman, thankful that simply by jogging ahead of him, she'd brought him back to the present and out of a near clash with the crippling anxiety he refused to let get the better of him.

As he put distance between him and the woman in pink, he passed the shadow of a building. A movement out of the corner of his eye made him spin around. He jogged in a circle, his pulse ratcheting up, his body ready, instincts on high alert. The scuffle of feet made him circle again and stop. He crouched in a fighting stance and faced the threat, the memory of his abduction exploding in his mind, slamming him back to Somalia, back to the dry terrain of Africa and the twenty rebels who'd jumped him and Dane when they'd been leading a training exercise in the bush.

Instead of Somali militants garbed in camouflage and turbans, a small child darted out of his parents' reach and ran past Wyatt, headed toward the edge of the river.

His mother screamed, "Johnnie, stop!"

By the time Wyatt grasped that the child wasn't an al-Shabab fighter, the kid had nearly reached the edge.

Wyatt lunged for the boy and grabbed him by the scruff of the neck as the little guy tripped. Johnnie would have gone headfirst into the slow-moving, shallow water had Wyatt not snagged him at the last minute.

Instead of thanking Wyatt, the kid kicked, wiggled and squirmed until Wyatt was forced to set the boy on the ground. Then Johnnie planted the tip of his shoe in Wyatt's shin with razor-sharp precision.

Wyatt released him and bent to rub the sore spot.

Little Johnnie ran back to his mother, who wrapped her arms around the brat and cooed. Safe in his mother's arms, he glared at Wyatt.

Wyatt frowned, the ache in his shin nothing compared to the way his heart raced all over again.

The boy's mother gave Wyatt an apologetic wince and hugged her baby boy to her chest. "Thank you."

A small crowd had gathered, more because Wyatt, the parents and child blocked the sidewalk than because they were interested in a man who'd just rescued a child from a potential drowning.

His heartbeat racing, his palms clammy and his pulse pounding so loudly in his ears he couldn't hear anything else, Wyatt nodded, glancing around for an escape. Fuck! What was wrong with him? If he didn't get away quickly, he'd succumb this time. Where was the woman in the pink shorts when he needed her? Some of his panic attacks had been so intense he'd actually thought he was having a heart attack. He hadn't told his commander, or the psychologist assigned to his case, for fear of setting back his reassignment even further. He wanted to be back in the field where the action was. Where he was fighting a real enemy, not himself.

As it was, he'd been given this snowbird task of heading up the security for the International Trade Convention. "Do this job, prove you're one hundred percent and we'll take it from there," Captain Ketchum had said. To Wyatt, it sounded like a load of bullshit with no promises.

Hell, any trained monkey could provide security for a bunch of businessmen. What did Ketchum think Wyatt could add to the professional security firm hired to man the exits and provide a visual deterrent to pickpockets and vagrants?

Wyatt had tried to see the assignment from his commander's point of view. He was a soldier barely recovered from a shitload of injuries caused by violent militants who set no value on life, limb and liberty. Sure, he'd been so close to death he almost prayed for it, but he was back as good as—

A twinge in his knee, made it buckle. Rather than fall in front of all those people, Wyatt swung around like he meant it and stepped out smartly.

And barreled into the woman he'd been following. Her head down, intent on moving, she'd been squeezing past him at that exact moment.

The female staggered sideways, her hands flailing in the air as she reached out to grab something to hold onto. When her fingers only met air, she toppled over the edge and fell into the river with a huge splash.

Another lady screamed and the crowd that had been standing on the sidewalk rushed to the edge of the river, pushing Wyatt forward to the point he almost went in with the woman.

A dark, wet head rose from the water like an avenging Titan, spewing curses. She pushed lank strands of hair from her face and glared up at him. "Are you just going to stand there and stare? Or are you going to get me out of this?"

Guilt and the gentleman in Wyatt urged him

to hold out his hand to her. She grasped it firmly and held on as he pulled her out of the river and onto the sidewalk. She was so light, he yanked with more force than necessary and she fell against him, her tight little wet body pressing against his.

His arm rose to her waist automatically, holding her close until she was steady on her own feet.

The redhead stared up into his eyes, her own green ones wide, sparkling with anger, her pretty little mouth shaped in an O.

At this close range, Wyatt saw the freckles sprinkled across her nose. Instead of making her face appear flawed, they added to her beauty, making her more approachable, though not quite girl-next-door. She was entirely too sexy for that moniker. Especially all wet with her skin showing through the thin fabric of the lime green tank top.

Then she was pushing against him—all business and righteous anger.

A round of applause sounded behind him, though he didn't deserve it since he'd knocked her into the water in the first place. "My apologies, darlin'."

She fished the MP3 out of the strap around her arm and pressed the buttons on it, shaking her head. "Well, that one's toast."

"Sweetheart, I'll buy you a new one," Wyatt said, giving her his most charming smile. "Just give me your name and number so that I can find you to replace it."

"No thanks. I'm not your sweetheart and I don't have time to deal with it." She squeezed the water out of her hair and turned away, dropping the MP3 into a trashcan.

With her body shape imprinted in dank river water on his vest and PT shorts, he was reluctant to let her leave without finding out her name. "At least let me know your name."

She hesitated, opened her mouth to say something, then she shook her head as if thinking better of it. "Sorry, I've gotta go." She shrugged free of his grip and took off, disappearing into the throng of tourists on the River Walk.

Wyatt would have jogged after her, but the number of people on the sidewalk made it impossible for a big guy like him to ease his way through. Regret tugged at his gut. Although he hadn't made the best first impression on her, her bright green eyes and tight little body had given him the first twinge of lust he'd felt since he'd been in Somalia. Perhaps being on snowbird detail would help him get his mojo back. At the very least, he might find time, and a willing woman, to get laid. Okay, so a few days of R&R in a cushy assignment might not be too bad.

A flash of pretty green eyes haunted his every step as he wove his way through the thickening crowd to his hotel where he'd stashed his duffel bag. He wondered if in an entire city of people he'd manage to run into the red-haired jogger again. If so, maybe he could refrain from knocking her into the river next time and instead get her number.

Fiona Allen arrived at the door to her hotel room, dripping wet and in need of a shower to rinse off the not-so-sanitary San Antonio River water. She couldn't afford to come down with some disease this week. Not when dignitaries were already arriving for the International Trade Convention due to kick off in less than two days' time.

If she did come down with something, it would all be that big, hulking, decidedly sexy, beast of a man's fault. The one who'd knocked her into the river in the first place. When he'd pulled her out with one hand, he'd barely strained.

Her heart had raced when he'd slammed her up against his chest. She blamed it on the shock of being thrown into the river, but she suspected the solid wall of muscles she'd rested her hands against had more to do with it.

For a brief moment, she'd remained dumb-struck and utterly attracted to the clumsy stranger. Had it been any other circumstance and she hadn't been covered in river slime, she might have asked for his number. *Yeah, right.*

As the convention coordinator, she couldn't afford to date or be sick, or for anything to go wrong while thousands of businessmen and politicians attended the meetings. She'd been hired by the city to ensure this event went off without a hitch, and she wouldn't let a single disgruntled employee, terrorist or hulking body-builder knock her off her game. No sir. She had all the plans locked up tighter than Fort Knox and the hired staff marching to the beat of her military-style drum.

She wasn't the daughter of an Army colonel for nothing. She knew discipline; hard work and using your brain couldn't be replaced by help from sexy strangers with insincere apologies. If this convention was going to be a success, it would be so based on all of her hard work in the planning stages.

Once inside her room, she headed straight for the bathroom and twisted the knob on the shower, amazed at how much her breasts still tingled after being smashed against the broad chest of the clumsy oaf who'd knocked her into the river. She shook her head, attributing the tingling to the chill of the air conditioning unit.

In the bathroom, she stripped her damp gym shorts and tank top, dropping the soaked mess into a plastic bag. She'd hand it over to the hotel staff and ask them to launder them, otherwise she'd have nothing to work out in. Who was she kidding? She wouldn't need to work out once the convention began.

Fiona unclipped her bra and slid out of her panties, adding them to the bag of dirty clothes. Then she stepped beneath the shower's spray and attacked her body with shampoo and citrus-scented soap. Images of the muscle man on the River Walk resurfaced, teasing her body into a lather that had nothing to do with the bar of soap. Too bad her time wasn't her own. The man had certainly piqued her interest. Not that she'd find him again in a city of over a million people.

As she slid her soap-covered hand over her breast, she paused to tweak a nipple and moaned. It had been far too long since she'd been with a man. She'd have to do something about that soon. With her, a little sex went a long way. Perhaps she would test the batteries in her vibrator and make do with pleasuring herself. Although the device was cold and couldn't give her all she wanted, it was a lot less messy in so very many ways. Relationships required work. Building a business had taken all of her time.

Fiona trailed her hand down her belly to the tuft of curls over her mons and sighed. Maybe she'd find a man. After the convention when her life wasn't nearly as crazy. She rinsed, switched off the water and stepped out on the mat, her core pulsing, her clit throbbing, needy and unfulfilled.

With a lot of items still begging for her attention, she couldn't afford the luxury of standing beneath the hot spray of the massaging showerhead, masturbating. Towel in hand, she rubbed her skin briskly, her breasts tingling at the thought of the big guy on the River Walk.

By the time the convention was over, that man could be long gone. He probably was a businessman passing through, or one of the military men on temporary duty. Even if he lived in the city, what were the chances of running into him again? Slim to none. San Antonio was a big place with a lot of people.

Well, damn. She should have given him her name and number. A quick fling would get her over her lust cravings and back to her laser-sharp focus.

She dragged a brush through her long, curly hair, wishing she'd cut it all off. With the convention taking all of her spare time, she didn't have time to waste on taming her mane of cursed curls. Most of the time it was the bane of her existence, requiring almost an hour of steady work with the straightener to pull the curls out. Having left her clean clothes in the drawer in the bedroom, Fiona stood naked in front of the mirror as she blew her hair dry, coaxing it around a large round brush.

This convention was her shot at taking her business international. If she succeeded and pulled off the biggest event of her career without a hitch, other jobs would come her way on her own merit, not based on a recommendation from one of her stepfather's cronies.

When she'd graduated with her masters in Operations Management, she'd invested the money her mother had left her in her business, F.A. International Event Planner. Since then, she'd steadily built her client list from companies based in San Antonio. Starting out with weddings, parties and small gigs, she'd established a reputation for attention to detail and an ability to follow through. She'd worked her way in as a consultant for some of the larger firms in the area when they'd needed to plan a convention based in San Antonio.

Finally she'd gotten a lead on the International Trade Convention and had applied. Her stepfather put a bug in the ear of one of his buddies from his active Army days at the Pentagon and she'd landed the contract.

Now all she had to do was prove she was up to the task. If it fell apart, she'd lose her business, disgrace the U.S. government and shame her stepfather. The pressure to succeed had almost been overwhelming. To manage the workload, she'd taken out a big loan, more than doubled her staff, coordinated the use of the convention center, arranged for all the food, meeting rooms, audio-visual equipment, translators, and blocked out lodging and security for the guests.

As she dried her hair, she stared at the shadows beneath her eyes. Only a few more sleepless nights and the convention would be underway and over. She'd be playing the role of orchestra conductor, managing the staff to ensure everything was perfect. The most important aspect of the event was tight security. The Department of Homeland Security had notified her today that with all the foreign delegates scheduled to attend, the probability of a terrorist attack had risen to threat level orange.

A quick glance at her watch reminded her that she only had ten minutes to get ready before her meeting in the lounge with the man Homeland Security had insisted she add to her staff to oversee security. This last-minute addition made her nervous. She knew nothing about the man, his background or his capabilities. He could prove more of a hindrance than a help if he got in the way. All she knew was that he'd better be on time, and he'd better be good. With a hundred items roiling around in her head at any one moment, the last thing she needed was an international incident.

Fiona shut off the blow dryer, ran the brush through her hair and reached for the doorknob, reminding herself to look at the e-mail on her laptop from Homeland Security to get the name of the contact she'd be meeting shortly. Before she could turn the doorknob, it twisted in her hand and the door flew open.

A very naked man, with wild eyes and bared teeth shoved her up against the wall, pinned her wrists above her head and demanded, "Who the hell are you? And why are you in my room?"

Read the rest of Wyatt's War

ABOUT THE AUTHOR

ELLE JAMES also writing as MYLA JACKSON is a *New York Times* and *USA Today* Bestselling author of books including cowboys, intrigues and paranormal adventures that keep her readers on the edges of their seats. With over eighty works in a variety of sub-genres and lengths she has published with Harlequin, Samhain, Ellora's Cave, Kensington, Cleis Press, and Avon. When she's not at her computer, she's traveling, snow skiing, boating, or riding her ATV, dreaming up new stories. Learn more about Elle James at www.ellejames.com

Website | Facebook | Twitter | GoodReads | Newsletter | BookBub | Amazon

Or visit her alter ego Myla Jackson at mylajackson.com
Website | Facebook | Twitter | Newsletter

Follow Me!

www.ellejames.com
ellejames@ellejames.com

ALSO BY ELLE JAMES

Brotherhood Protectors Series

Montana SEAL (#1)

Bride Protector SEAL (#2)

Montana D-Force (#3)

Cowboy D-Force (#4)

Montana Ranger (#5)

Montana Dog Soldier (#6)

Montana SEAL Daddy (#7)

Montana Ranger's Wedding Vow (#8)

Montana SEAL Undercover Daddy (#9)

Cape Cod SEAL Rescue (#10)

Montana SEAL Friendly Fire (#11)

Montana SEAL's Bride (#11) TBD

Montana Rescue

Hot SEAL, Salty Dog

Hearts & Heroes Series

Wyatt's War (#1)

Mack's Witness (#2)

Hot Combat (#1)

Hot Target (#2)

Hot Zone (#3)

Hot Velocity (#4)

Texas Billionaire Club

Tarzan & Janine (#1)

Something To Talk About (#2)

Who's Your Daddy (#3)

Love & War (#4)

Hellfire Series

Hellfire, Texas (#1)

Justice Burning (#2)

Smoldering Desire (#3) TBD

Up in Flames (#4) TBD

Hellfire in High Heels (#5) TBD

Cajun Magic Mystery Series

Voodoo on the Bayou (#1)

Voodoo for Two (#2)

Deja Voodoo (#3)

Cajun Magic Mysteries Books 1-3

Nick of Time

Alaskan Fantasy

Blown Away

Warrior's Conquest

Rogues

Enslaved by the Viking Short Story

Conquests

Smokin' Hot Firemen

Love on the Rocks

Protecting the Colton Bride

Heir to Murder

Secret Service Rescue

High Octane Heroes

Haunted

Engaged with the Boss

Cowboy Brigade

Time Raiders: The Whisper

Bundle of Trouble

Killer Body

Operation XOXO

An Unexpected Clue

Baby Bling

Under Suspicion, With Child

CPSIA information can be obtained
at www.ICGtesting.com
Printed in the USA
LVHW080713240722
724265LV00024B/509

9 781626 951600